"I brought you something."

Josiah held out two mason jars. One was empty and the other was filled with long screws. He explained that each evening before Will went to bed, he could take one of the screws from the clear mason jar and put it into the blue mason jar. "When you run out of screws in the clear jar, that's when your *mamm* will come home."

"But the blue jar doesn't have any screws in it at all." Will looked upset.

"You're right. How many nights have you been here?"

The boy glanced at Anke. "Five," she said. "Do you need me to help you count them out?"

"*Jah.* I can only count in *Englisch*," he replied.

Anke couldn't stop smiling. How she felt reminded her of the day her father had hung the swing in the tree for Clara. Her mother was delighted to see her young daughter enjoying herself so much. She never forgot that her mother had told her, *The way to a man's heart might be through his* bauch, *but the way to a woman's heart is through her* kind.

Now Anke knew exactly what she'd meant. Not that she thought Will was her child or that Josiah was trying to win her heart. But what he did for her nephew was so sweet she hummed her way through the morning.

Carrie Lighte lives in Massachusetts next door to a Mennonite farming family, and she frequently spots deer, foxes, fisher cats, coyotes and turkeys in her backyard. Having enjoyed traveling to several Amish communities in the eastern United States, she looks forward to visiting settlements in the western states and in Canada. When she's not reading, writing or researching, Carrie likes to hike, kayak, bake and play word games.

Visit the Author Profile page at LoveInspired.com.

Caring for Her Amish Family

Carrie Lighte

LOVE INSPIRED
INSPIRATIONAL ROMANCE

LOVE INSPIRED®
INSPIRATIONAL ROMANCE

Recycling programs for this product may not exist in your area.

ISBN-13: 978-1-335-56749-9

Caring for Her Amish Family

This edition published by arrangement with Harlequin Books S.A.

For questions and comments about the quality of this book, please contact us at CustomerService@Harlequin.com.

Love Inspired
22 Adelaide St. West, 41st Floor
Toronto, Ontario M5H 4E3, Canada
www.LoveInspired.com

Printed in U.S.A.

Be ye therefore merciful, as your Father also is merciful. Judge not, and ye shall not be judged: condemn not, and ye shall not be condemned.
—*Luke* 6:36–37

For my dad, who keeps his word

Chapter One

At twenty-seven, Anke Bachman was a year older than her sister-in-law, yet Velda was lecturing her in the same tone she used to admonish her four little children.

"You know what the Bible says, Anke. Whoever is a friend of the world is the enemy of *Gott*." She furiously scraped the remnants of mashed potatoes from the inside of a large pot with a spatula.

"*Jah*, that's true," Anke replied. "Yet it also says that people who don't provide for their own *familye* have denied their faith."

"But your *schweschder* left our *familye*!" Velda emphatically waved the spatula in the air, splattering little blobs of potatoes on the floor. Her husband, Ernest—who was Anke's brother—was as calm as Velda was excitable. Seated at the table, he was quietly sipping tea and eating a second slice of sour-milk cake. The little ones had been so tired they'd gone to bed immediately after supper, but Anke feared her sister-in-law's voice would wake them again as she exclaimed, "And Clara didn't just leave our *familye*, she left our faith!"

Anke didn't need a reminder: she'd been lamenting her youngest sister's rebellious lifestyle ever since Clara ran away during her *rumspringa* a little over five years ago. In all that time, there wasn't a day that went by when Anke didn't pray that Clara would repent and return to her family's home in New Hope, Maine. Or at the very least that she'd call or write to let them know she was okay.

Her prayers were finally answered last week when her sister sent a letter requesting Anke meet her on Saturday in a little diner on the edge of town. "Please come alone," she'd written. "I have something very important to discuss with you."

For days after receiving the note, Anke was filled with hope that Clara wanted to discuss coming back to her Amish community. The possibility made her so ecstatic that her feet barely touched the ground.

But that was before Anke had seen her.

And it was before she'd heard Clara's story. When they'd met, Anke almost hadn't recognized her sister. Clara's flaxen hair was cut shorter than a boy's and streaked purple. Her ears were pierced six or seven times, she had a tiny gold hoop in one nostril and she was wearing ripped jeans and a hooded black sweatshirt. But even more alarming than her accessories or clothes was how old and hardened her face had appeared. Her eyelids were so puffy that her baby-blue eyes looked half the size they used to be. Or maybe that was because she was scowling.

She'd allowed Anke to hug her for a long time, but Clara hadn't returned her embrace. When Anke had finally let go, her eyes brimming with tears, Clara had swiftly stepped to the other side of the table. Gesturing to the middle-aged dark-haired *Englisch* woman seated at the booth, she'd announced, "This is Yolanda, my sponsor."

"Sponsor?" Anke had repeated numbly, trying to understand why Clara had invited a third person to meet with them when she'd specifically requested that Anke come there alone.

Clara quickly delved into an account of what she'd been doing since she'd left home, admitting she'd originally run away because she'd become pregnant during her *rumspringa*. Four months later, she gave birth to a baby boy she named Will. She and her *Englisch* boyfriend were together until about a year ago, when he'd broken up with her and moved to California, claiming he was too young to be a dad and he didn't want anything to do with her or their child.

After he left, Clara had been so sad and lonely that she'd turned to alcohol for comfort. It didn't take long before she was addicted. Her drinking had led to such irresponsible behavior that a judge had told her if she didn't participate in a residential recovery program, she'd have to put Will in foster care.

Although Clara had recited the details of her life as unfeelingly as if she'd been reading items off a grocery list, they were so painful and shocking for Anke to hear that she'd struggled not to wince.

Dear Gott, *you've brought my* schweschder *and me together again for a reason*, she'd silently prayed as Clara was speaking. *Please help me respond to her in accordance with Your will, no matter how disappointed I am in her behavior.*

After hearing Clara's story, Anke assumed the reason she'd wanted to meet with her was because she needed money. Anke didn't know how much a residential recovery program cost—she wasn't even sure what it was. But she did understand what it felt like to be separated from one's child. Granted, Clara wasn't actually Anke's daughter, but she had raised the girl after their parents died when a car rear-ended their buggy nine years ago. Even though Anke's and Clara's circumstances were completely different, Anke didn't want her sister to have to endure the kind of heartache Anke had suffered when Clara had run away.

"I've been making aprons and putting them on consignment at Millers' Restaurant, so I've built up a savings account. It's not a lot, but you can have it all," she'd offered. "If you agree to let me tell our *bruder* about your predicament—he might be willing to help, too."

"I don't need your money. I'm not a *beggar*," Clara had snapped. She'd sat back against the booth seat and crossed her arms over her chest, clearly offended.

"Maybe not, Clara, but you *are* in need," Yolanda had interjected pointedly. Anke hadn't understood what she'd meant, but her remark seemed to have an effect on Clara's attitude.

For the first time since she'd arrived in the diner, Anke had caught a glimpse of how vulnerable her little sister really was. Her voice quavering, she'd said, "I'm sorry. I appreciate the offer, but the costs are covered by the state. What I really need is for you to watch Will while I'm in the program. It's only for six weeks. Please, Anke? I'm desperate. I don't want him to wind up with strangers. What if I never get him back?"

That's exactly how I've *felt all these years* you've *been away*, Anke thought. She'd told Clara she'd have to pray about it. She'd also have to discuss it with Ernest and Velda since they all lived in the same house.

The dwelling was technically Anke's; as the eldest sibling, she'd inherited it the year her parents died. But Ernest and Velda had been living in it with her ever since they got married, and Anke considered it as much theirs as hers. She couldn't have possibly made a major decision that would affect their entire household without consulting them first.

She'd anticipated that Velda would have reservations, but she hadn't expected her to get worked up into such a tizzy. Trying to show her sister-in-law she understood her concerns, Anke started to say, "Clara was on *rumspringa* when she left, so she's not under the *bann*, but—"

Hands on her hips, Velda interrupted, "That doesn't mean we should *wilkom* her with open arms! Especially since she hasn't indicated any interest in repenting and putting her *Englisch* lifestyle behind her."

"Please allow me to finish expressing my

thought," Anke replied softly. "What I was going to say was that even though Clara was on *rumspringa* and she isn't under the *bann*, I don't approve of the way she's been living any more than you do. And *neh*, she hasn't indicated an intention to leave the *Englisch*."

Anke paused, thinking, *She hasn't even really admitted remorse—I get the sense she's only going into the recovery program because she has to.* But her prayer was that the Lord would change Clara's heart, as well as her actions. She continued, "However, I'm not asking you and Ernest to *wilkom* her back into our home. I'm asking you to help me watch her *suh* here for six weeks. What his *mamm* has done isn't *his* fault. And there's nothing in our *Ordnung* which would prohibit us from providing a temporary home for him, considering his age and circumstances."

Velda spluttered. "The only reason there's nothing in our *Ordnung* prohibiting it is because the situation has never *kumme* up before! And that's because everyone knows better than to invite *Englischers* to live in one's home."

"The Nisley *familye* rents out their *daadi haus* to *Englischers* for three months during fishing season," Anke reminded her.

"*Jah,* but that's not the same as breaking bread with them day after day," Velda countered. "I don't want an *Englisch bu* introducing our impressionable *kinner* to the temptations of the *Englisch* world."

"I understand your concern, Velda," Anke responded sincerely. "But Will is five years old, so he's impressionable, too. It's possible that your *kinner* might demonstrate the virtues of *our* faith to him. And perhaps by caring for Clara's *suh*, we'll win her back to our *familye*."

Having finished his cake, Ernest put down his fork, wiped his mouth with a napkin and finally spoke. "I want Clara to return, too, Anke. But I'm also very concerned about the influence Will might have on our household. Just because it's permissible for him to stay with us doesn't mean it's advisable. I believe we ought to do what we *know* is best for our household, instead of what we *hope* might turn out best for our *schweschder* and her *suh*."

Although her brother's reasoning made sense, Anke wasn't ready to give up. She didn't want to push Ernest and Velda to violate their consciences, but neither could she ignore her strong belief that caring for Will was the Godly thing to do. *If we lived in separate* heiser, *this wouldn't be an issue*, she thought.

Suddenly, she was struck with a solution that seemed so obvious she didn't know why it hadn't occurred to her sooner. "I could stay in the *daadi haus* with Will!"

"That place isn't fit for you and a *kind*," Ernest objected. "Even *I* wouldn't want to sleep in there, especially not in February."

Situated on the northern corner of the property, the little structure had been home to Anke and Ernest's grandparents before they died some fifteen years ago. On occasion since then, the Bachmans had used the small dwelling for visiting relatives they didn't have room to accommodate in the main house, such as when Ernest and Velda got married. However, two years after the wedding, a tree limb fell on the roof and the damage had been patched over, but not thoroughly repaired. The inside of the house needed restoration, too.

But Anke had already come up with the perfect plan. "I'll have a frolic on *Samschdaag*. The *menner* can repair the roof and the *weibsleit* can help me clean it inside. It'll be nice and cozy when Will arrives next *Muundaag*."

"All the available *menner* are helping Omer Wilford build his workshop this *Samschdaag*, remember?"

"Oh, that's right. The *weibsleit* are having a quilting bee at Lena's, so they won't be available to help me, either." Anke tentatively proposed, "Would you be comfortable allowing

Will to stay in this *haus* with us until the following *Samschdaag*?"

"*Neh*," Velda objected vehemently. "I wouldn't be comfortable with that at all."

Ernest agreed with his wife's sentiment. "It's okay if our *kinner* play with Will on occasion, but staying at our *haus* for five nights? That doesn't seem prudent. What if he grows too accustomed to us and then doesn't want to leave to go live in the *daadi haus*? It will be upsetting for him as well as for our *kinner*."

Anke bit her lip, refusing to be defeated. It dawned on her that she could withdraw the money from her savings account and pay someone to work on fixing the place up during the week. Surely there was someone in the New Hope community who needed an income as much as she needed his carpentry services. "All right, I'll find someone who's willing and able to make repairs to the roof before Will arrives."

"Like who? Your suitor Keith Harnish?" Velda boldly inquired, even though most of the Amish in New Hope generally didn't discuss who they were dating, not even with their family members.

"Keith is *not* my suitor," Anke insisted. Although it was true that she had agreed to walk out with him about a month ago, she'd quickly decided it had been a mistake to say yes to his persistent requests to court. Like the other two men who'd courted her in her lifetime, he just didn't seem to understand that caring for her family took priority over going bowling on Saturday night or for a buggy ride on Sunday afternoon. She'd felt that way when she was raising Clara, and she felt that way about helping Ernest and Velda care for her nieces and nephews, too. Anke didn't blame any of her suitors for feeling frustrated with her; they wanted to get married and have their own families, not play second fiddle to hers. She'd come to realize it wasn't fair to a man for her to accept an offer of courtship, knowing she had little time or inclination to develop a relationship with him.

That was especially true now, because until Clara completed her recovery program, Anke's primary focus was going to be giving Will a healthy, happy, loving Amish home. In fact, in this instance she believed her singleness was a gift from the Lord. *If I had kinner of my own, I might be as protective of them as Ernest and Velda are of their brood*, she thought. *And then who would care for little Will?*

"Don't look so embarrassed," Velda teased, clearly in a better mood now that she could rest assured her *Englisch* nephew wouldn't be living in the same house as her children. "Every *weibsmensch* needs a little romance in her life."

Not me, Anke thought. *All I need is a* gut *carpenter—and preferably one who can start working on the* daadi haus *right away.*

"We're sure having one fierce cold snap," Josiah Mast's brother Victor remarked on Tuesday afternoon as his horse pulled the buggy onto the main road leading toward the New Hope bus station. It was the same station Victor had picked Josiah up at when he'd arrived yesterday; now they were headed back there so Victor could catch a bus to Upstate New York. "At this rate, the ground won't thaw until July. I'm *hallich* you're here, but for your sake, you probably should have waited until April to *kumme.*"

Josiah had moved from a small district near Arthur, Illinois, to New Hope to work for his brother, who owned a fence-installation business. He was aware that Victor wouldn't have any customer orders to fill until the weather warmed, but Josiah was eager to relocate to Maine. "I actually think this timing works out well for all of us. I'll be here to care for your livestock while you and Laura are away. And

I can lay your new floor in the kitchen without worrying I'm getting underfoot."

Last week, Laura, Victor's wife, had rushed to Upstate New York after her father suffered a stroke. Now that it was clear she'd need to extend her stay to help during his recovery period, Victor was going to join her. So Josiah would be staying alone in their house in New Hope.

"It's *wunderbaar* that you'll be working on the floor while we're gone, but won't you feel lonely here on your own?"

"*Neh*, I'll be fine." Actually Josiah was looking forward to some solitude, especially after feeling as if he'd spent the past year under scrutiny from both the *Englischers* and the Amish in his community.

It all began last winter on a day a lot like this one, when he was traveling past a golf course and he spied his girlfriend Jana's sixteen-year-old brother, Stanley. The teenager and a couple of his *Englisch* pals were standing around a bonfire, watching their friends take turns racing snowmobiles nearby. Aware they were trespassing and they might get into trouble with the police, Josiah had pulled over to offer Stanley a ride home.

To his consternation, when he got out of the buggy, Josiah noticed the teenager had alcohol on his breath. Stanley was on his *rumspringa* so the church might not have held him accountable for this transgression. However, his father, Emery, was a deacon and he didn't tolerate alcohol consumption by anyone under any circumstances. Understandably, Stanley seemed chagrined to have been caught drinking and he refused to go home.

Josiah was just about to get back into his buggy when he heard a loud shout: one of the passengers had fallen off the snowmobile. The driver just pumped his fist in the air and sped off, causing the *Englischers* standing near the bonfire to laugh, without any apparent concern for the passenger's well-being. So Josiah ran down the hill to see if the youth was okay. He was, but he'd twisted his ankle and Josiah had to assist him back to the bonfire.

Meanwhile, someone must have notified the golf club manager that there were trespassers on the property, because he'd arrived in his car. By the time Josiah returned to the group, the manager was interrogating the kids—one of whom was his own son—about where they'd purchased the alcohol.

I told you what would happen if I caught you using a fake ID again! He'd yelled at his son, a blond boy who looked deceptively innocent.

I didn't buy it or use a fake ID, Dad. That

Amish guy over there—Josiah—told us he had beer in the back of his buggy and he'd look the other way if we wanted to help ourselves. We've only had a few sips.

Josiah had been almost as shocked to hear the *Englisch* kid refer to him by name as he was by his outrageous lie. *I've never purchased or transported alcohol in my life,* he'd said to the boy's father. *But you can take a look in the carriage and see for yourself there's nothing in there except a toolbox.*

The manager had climbed into the buggy and peered over the seat. He'd reached in and pulled out a half-empty bottle of gin and a six-pack of beer. Holding them up, he'd asked, *These aren't yours?*

Josiah had been appalled. Neh. *Absolutely not.* He hadn't wanted to come right out and accuse the guy's son of stashing the alcohol there when they saw the manager's car approaching. For all he knew, it could have been Stanley who'd done it. In any case, Josiah hadn't actually witnessed them doing it and God's Word warned against bearing false witness about one's neighbor. All he knew for certain was that it wasn't *his.*

Fortunately, the manager had seemed to surmise what was going on. He'd told Josiah he'd get to the bottom of the matter with the teens and their parents and assured him the youth would face consequences for their behavior. He'd offered to bring them to Josiah's house to apologize for lying once they'd sobered up, but Josiah had said it wasn't necessary and he hadn't supplied his address. He'd just wanted to leave with Stanley.

Make sure you don't come back here again, the manager had warned the teenager. *Or I'll pay your elders a visit and let them know what you've been up to.*

Clearly the *Englischer* had a strong understanding of how to intimidate an Amish boy—Josiah had seen by how nervous Stanley was that he wouldn't make the same mistake twice. So on the way home, he'd promised that if Stanley agreed he'd never drink or trespass again, Josiah wouldn't tell anyone about what he'd done or where he'd been.

However, Josiah later discovered that someone had videoed the entire episode on a cell phone and it went "viral," as the *Englisch* would say. Both Stanley and Josiah worked for Emery in his door-making shop and before long a customer came in and played the clip for the three of them.

Astonishingly, Emery demonstrated less faith in Josiah than the golf club manager had shown him. After the customer left, Emery hadn't even asked to hear Josiah's side of the story before reproaching him. *You know our* Ordnung *prohibits drinking any alcohol whatsoever!*

Trying not to respond in anger, Josiah had stated evenly, *It wasn't mine—I believe the kids put those bottles in my carriage because they saw the manager coming and they didn't want to be caught red-handed.*

Emery had then turned to Stanley and questioned, *Is it true? Did the* Englischers *put the bottles in Josiah's buggy?* Josiah noticed he'd automatically assumed it was the *Englischers*, and not his son, who had been drinking.

The teenager had somberly shaken his head. *If they did, I didn't see them do it.*

On one hand, Josiah understood Stanley's reluctance to snitch on his friends and to face the consequences of his own behavior, too. On the other hand, he was disgusted. Didn't the teenager have any conscience at all?

Emery had turned his attention back to grilling Josiah. *If you had nothing to hide, why didn't you tell me about this incident yourself? Why did I find out about it from an* Englischer?

Josiah had hesitated in order to give Stanley a chance to speak up. He'd hoped the boy would have confessed the real reason Josiah never reported the incident to Emery, but Stanley had just silently looked down at his feet.

The club manager knew their claim didn't have any merit and he assured me he'd hold the kids accountable for their drinking. As far as I was concerned, the matter was over, so there was no need to mention it, Josiah had said at last.

But he knew how feeble his excuse sounded. Emery hadn't come right out and said he didn't believe him, but the older man began giving Josiah the cold shoulder. He must have told others in their district about it, because Josiah sensed some of them looking askance at him, too. It disappointed him, but not nearly as much as Jana's response did.

I know you don't drink, so you must have been hiding the alcohol for someone else, weren't you? she'd asked after Emery told her about what had happened. *Is it someone in our district? Or was it for your sister's husband— they were visiting from Ohio last week, weren't they?*

Josiah was angry she hadn't believed him and appalled she'd assumed the alcohol belonged to someone in *his* family. He'd considered telling her about her brother's drinking. Yet no matter how irresponsible and cowardly Stanley's behavior was, Josiah couldn't break his word to him. After all, God was always faithful to *His* promises and Josiah wanted to try his best to follow the Lord's example. However, he had decided he couldn't court someone who didn't have more trust in him than what Jana had demonstrated, so he'd broken up with her.

Shortly afterward, Emery said he no longer needed Josiah's services. He'd claimed it was because business was slow, but Josiah believed the real reason was that the video had received so much attention, so more and more customers recognized him when they came into the shop. (It wasn't difficult, considering Josiah was one of only two men in the district who had red hair.) They'd whisper to each other, *Isn't he the one who was hanging out and drinking with the underage kids on the golf course?*

Josiah had hoped the whole fiasco would blow over and people would lose interest, but it seemed to drag on. Meanwhile, even the Amish business owners who believed he'd been telling the truth were reluctant to hire him because they were worried his notoriety would reflect poorly on them, too. As a result, for the past year Josiah had been taking whatever odd jobs he could get, so he was going to be strapped for cash until he began working for Victor.

"Do you know anyone who might be hiring?" he asked as his brother applied the buggy's brake and simultaneously slowed the horse in front of the bus station.

"*Neh*, but you can ask around at *kurrich* on *Sundaag*." Victor reached into the back to pull out his luggage. He and Josiah said goodbye and Victor hopped out of the buggy. But then he stuck his head back in for one last piece of advice. "The *leit* in New Hope are very friendly. The teenage youth attend singings, but there's another group closer to your age who go on outings together. Bowling, hiking, canoeing, they've even hiked Mount Katahdin together. I know they'd *wilkom* your company. When you go to *kurrich*, Honor Bawell will probably tell you all about their next outing."

Honor must be the community matchmaker, Josiah thought as he pulled out into traffic. There was one in every district, which was helpful if you were looking for a courtship, but he definitely wasn't. He'd recently turned twenty-five—the age when most Amish men he knew were married with two or three children. Josiah hadn't been in any rush; he'd wanted to wait until he'd met the right woman.

Unfortunately, I'm not a very gut *judge of character*, he thought.

Or more accurately, the problem was that *Jana* wasn't a good judge of character. She didn't know what kind of man Josiah really was and she had a huge blind spot in regard to her brother.

How could he have actually believed she might have been the Lord's intended for him? That she'd be the kind of spouse who'd support him through thick and thin, just as he would have done for her? In hindsight, Josiah was grateful they'd broken up before their courtship had progressed any further. And now that he thought about it, losing his job wasn't so bad, either; if Emery hadn't relieved him of his responsibilities, Josiah never would have moved to New Hope. Originally, he'd regretted having to leave Illinois. But now that he was here, he felt relieved that no one would question his commitment to following the *Ordnung* or wonder whether he or his loved ones had a drinking problem. This was going to be a fresh start.

Maybe by autumn, I'll have enough money to purchase lumber to build a small one-bedroom house on Laura and Victor's property, he thought. Instead of a *daadi haus*, it would be a bachelor *haus*; he could picture himself living alone there indefinitely.

The possibility energized him so much he decided to stop at the newly opened Amish hardware store to price some of the materials he'd need to put in a new kitchen floor for Laura. His brother had left him cash to pay for the supplies and wood, but he still intended to shop around for the best deal.

As he was browsing the aisles, he overheard an Amish woman talking to the man at the cash register. "I understand that you don't have the time to help me. And I'd really prefer someone from our *g'may* to work on the project. But since all of the skilled *menner* seem to be busy, too, I'll have to settle for an *Englisch* carpenter. So why won't you let me post an advertisement on the bulletin board by the door?"

Before the young man could reply, Josiah stepped forward. *"Guder nammigdaag,"* he greeted them both. "I'm Josiah Mast, Victor Mast's brother."

The man introduced himself as Keith Harnish, son of the hardware store owner.

Then the woman said, *"Wilkom* to New Hope, Josiah. My name is Anke Bachman." She had dark blond hair, blue-green eyes and ears that stuck out ever so slightly. He wouldn't have even noticed, except they were as pink as her cheeks; despite the soft smile she gave him, her flushed face indicated she was upset about something.

"It's *gut* to meet you both. I don't know if Victor mentioned I was coming to New Hope, but I've just moved here permanently. I overheard you saying you needed a carpenter. In Illinois I worked in a door-making shop and I'm looking for a temporary job until the spring, when I'll join my *bruder*'s crew installing fences. Can I ask what kind of project you need someone to do?"

Anke's smile grew wider. "*Jah.* I'll tell you all about it. Let's step outside so we can talk without disturbing Keith."

As they stood on the sidewalk in front of the store's big glass window, she told Josiah about her family's run-down *daadi haus*. From what he could understand, Anke's sister was undergoing some kind of treatment and she needed someone to care for her son while she was recovering in Portland, which was located about two hours south from New Hope. Anke's family's house was too small to accommodate everyone while the boy was in town, so Anke was going to stay in the *daadi haus* with him for the next six weeks or so.

"There's only one problem—we need to move into it on *Muundaag*. The rest of the repairs can be done over time, but by *Muundaag* we need a roof over our heads—one that doesn't leak, that is."

"From what you've described, I don't think that will be a problem," Josiah told her. They agreed on his hourly salary and he said he'd come to her house the following morning.

Denki, Lord, for providing for my need before I even expressed it, he silently prayed as Anke walked down the street. Then Josiah headed back into the hardware store to continue browsing.

"Did you tell her you'd repair the Bachmans' *daadi haus*?" Keith asked as soon as Josiah shut the door behind him.

"*Jah.* It's perfect timing, since I can't help my *bruder* install any fences until the weather warms," he replied. "And she seemed desperate. I'm surprised no one in the community wanted to take the job—or that her *familye* isn't hosting a frolic."

"Well, several of us might have made it a priority to help her, but because we don't agree with what she's doing..." Keith turned up his hands, as if there was no need to say more, but Josiah was completely confused.

"I don't understand. Is there a dispute over who owns the *daadi haus* or something?"

Keith snickered. "She didn't tell you about the controversy, did she? No wonder she wanted to speak with you about the project in private. She didn't want *me* to tell you, either."

"Tell me what? Is she doing something wrong? Is Anke violating the *Ordnung*?"

"Not exactly. But her *schweschder* Clara went *Englisch* five years ago. She had a *bobbel* out of wedlock and now she's an alcoholic. According to Anke's *schweschder*-in-law, Velda, the court is making Clara go into a program to get sober, so Anke is caring for Clara's *suh* for the six weeks—against her *familye*'s wishes. And against what many of us in the community believe she should do."

"I honestly had no idea her *schweschder* was an *Englischer*—or that she's an alcoholic," Josiah said, shaking his head in disbelief. "If I did, I would have had reservations about helping Anke, too. But I can't go back on my word now."

"Don't feel bad. It's not your fault. She should have been more forthcoming," Keith said. "But a word to the wise… Anke's very kind but sometimes her kindness clouds her better judgment. Be careful it doesn't cloud yours, too."

"I'll bear that in mind," Josiah solemnly replied, shaking his head in disbelief. How was it possible that he'd traveled over one thousand miles, only to find himself right back at square one?

Chapter Two

Anke hopped out of bed bright and early on Wednesday morning. She couldn't wait to get over to the *daadi haus* and begin cleaning it up. But first, she helped Velda make breakfast and serve it to the four children, all of whom were fussy eaters—except for Charity, the baby. At eight months old, she seemed to consume more than any of her three siblings. The twins, Millie and Micah, were barely four and they did almost everything together. Asher was almost six and next year he'd go to school, since that was when Amish children enrolled in first grade in New Hope. But for now, he was still home during the day. He was such a sweet boy that Anke couldn't help but hope he and Will would become friends, since Asher's behavior was more mature than the twins' was.

"Tell me about Victor's *bruder*," Velda said

as she wiped oatmeal from Charity's chin and forehead. "You told us you'd found someone to repair the *daadi haus* but then you dashed off to your room last night before I could ask any questions."

"That's because I'm working on a special apron order for a customer for Valentine's Day," Anke replied. It was also because she didn't want her sister-in-law to object to her hiring Josiah. Velda really shouldn't have had anything to say about the matter, since Anke was paying for his labor with her own money, but that wouldn't have stopped her from offering an opinion. Even though Velda had ultimately agreed it would be permissible for Will to stay with Anke in the *daadi haus*, Anke knew Velda's feathers were still ruffled about it.

She had undoubtedly complained about it to Keith's sister-in-law Ruth, who'd stopped by the house on Tuesday morning to drop off her daughter's hand-me-down clothes for Charity. Otherwise, how had Keith found out so quickly about Anke's intention to watch Will? She suspected if they'd still been courting, he would have gladly helped mend the *daadi haus* roof, but since she'd broken up with him, he'd said he didn't have time.

Oh, well. I don't need to figure out if he had

an ulterior motive for turning down the project, she thought. *I'm just grateful that the Lord provided for my needs through Josiah's help.*

Velda snapped her fingers in front of Anke's nose. "Are you awake? I asked you where Josiah lived before he moved here."

"Illinois, I think." Anke signaled Millie to close her mouth while she chewed her toast.

"Does he have a beard or mustache?"

Anke rolled her eyes. Amish men traditionally only grew beards after they were married; in Maine, they were also allowed to wear mustaches if they chose, although they weren't required to. So what Velda was really asking was whether he was single or not. Presumably, she didn't want the children to understand her question. *"Neh.* No beard." Before her sister-in-law could question her further, Anke added, "We didn't have a lot of time for chitchat. Mostly, I just described what I needed him to repair on the *daadi haus.*"

"Was he a carpenter when he lived in Illinois?"

"Kind of. He worked in a door-marking shop for four years and *kumme* spring, he's going to work for Victor installing fences. So I'm sure he can handle patching up a roof or replacing a few risers on the staircase, if that's what you're worried about."

"Why are you going to stay in the *daadi haus*?" Asher asked his aunt.

Anke, Ernest and Velda had agreed in advance they'd be as honest as was appropriate with the children about the situation. So yesterday during supper, they'd told them about Will's visit.

"Don't you remember what your *mamm* and *daed* and I told you?" Anke softly prodded. She'd noticed when Asher repeated explanations aloud in his own words, he absorbed them better. She started him off with a hint, "You have another *ant* you've never met..."

"And her name is *Ant* Clara. She was your little *schweschder* 'cept she went to live with the *Englisch*."

Millie chimed in, "That's something an Amish person should never, ever do."

"It's very, very bad." Micah shook his index finger with each word, just as Velda had done yesterday.

Although Anke understood why her sister-in-law had felt it was necessary to emphasize this point, she hoped her nephews and nieces wouldn't repeat it to Will. "*Jah*, but that's not your *gschwischderkind's* fault, so we aren't going to talk to him about it. Otherwise he might feel sad," she reminded them.

"*Jah*," Asher agreed. "And he's probably already sad because his *mamm* had to go to a special hospital. That's why you're going to take care of him—"

"Why can't his *daed* take care of him?" Millie interrupted her brother.

The adults hadn't addressed the topic of Will's father with the children yet. They weren't sure what the boy had been told, so they didn't want to present conflicting stories. However, now that Velda was put on the spot, she blurted out, "Will doesn't have a *daed*."

"Why not?" Millie pressed.

Micah tilted his head. "Did his *daed* die?"

"Well…" Velda had worked herself into a corner, so Anke knew she had to jump in.

"What your *mamm* meant was Will's *daed* is out of town. He's very far away, in a place called California. So I—"

Millie cut in, "Is his *daed Englisch*, too?"

"Jah," Anke answered matter-of-factly, hoping the less she said, the less she'd have to say. "So I get to take care of Will. Isn't that *wunderbaar*?"

"Jah. But why can't he stay in our *haus* with us? He can have my bed and I can sleep on cushions on the floor."

Asher's offer made Anke want to throw her arms around him. *If only your* mamm *were as welcoming as you are*, she thought.

"That's very generous of you, but Will's going to be here a long time. After a while, you'd get a crick in your neck from sleeping on the floor." Anke walked her fingers along her nephew's shoulder, up his neck and beneath his chin to tickle him.

"But we'll be able to play with him, right?"

"*Jah.* When your *mamm* allows you to."

Millie held up three fingers. "Is he coming in this many days?"

"*Neh*, in this many." Anke showed her there were five more days to go until Monday.

Velda stood up and started collecting the bowls. "You *kinner* go wash your hands and brush your teeth. I'll be there in a minute." Once they were out of earshot, she complained, "Will isn't even here yet and they're already so excited they hardly slept last night. Didn't I tell you having him here was going to be disruptive?"

"They're always this excited before their other *gschwischderkinner* visit, too," Anke said. "His *mamm* may have made some *baremlich* choices, but every *kind* deserves a warm *wilkom*. And every *kind* needs a warm *haus*. So if you'll excuse me, I'm going outside to wait for Josiah so we can walk over there together."

"Aren't you going to do the dishes? I need to help the children brush their teeth."

You're going to have to get used to running the household by yourself when I'm not here, Anke thought and then she immediately felt guilty. "*Jah.* I suppose there's no sense waiting out in the cold. I told Josiah to go ahead and stable his *gaul*, so I have a few minutes to spare."

"*Denki.*" Velda walked down the hall toward the bathroom, leaving Charity in her high chair.

"Ma-ma-ma-ma," the baby sang, banging a spoon on the tray. "Ma-ma-ma-ma."

Anke sang back to her as she washed and dried the dishes. When she finished and there was still no sign of Velda, she lifted the toddler from her chair. "Up you go, my little dumpling. Uh-oh. You *schtinke*—I need to change your *windel*."

"Da-da. Da-da," Charity babbled as Anke carried her upstairs to get a fresh cloth diaper. Velda and the children passed her on the way down. Apparently she'd been reading them a story. "I have to get going but Charity needs a fresh *windel*—"

"Okay." Velda smiled. "*Kumme* find me in the kitchen when you're done. I need a second cup of *kaffi*—do you want one?"

Neh, I need you to change Charity, Anke thought and once again, she felt guilty for being so irritable. Changing a diaper only took a few seconds; it wasn't as if Josiah was going to turn around and leave if she wasn't at the *daadi haus* exactly at eight o'clock, as they'd agreed.

On the contrary, when she came downstairs, Anke found him standing near the door in the kitchen, drinking a mug of coffee that Velda apparently had poured for him. She was across the room, leaning against the counter as they conversed, while the children stood off to the side, shyly looking up at their tall visitor.

Asher seemed especially awed, and Anke couldn't blame him. Josiah had removed his hat and his dark red curls—unusual for an Amish person in this part of the country— were eye-catching. Although he had baby blue eyes and a boyish spray of freckles across his wide forehead and cheeks, he appeared more commanding than juvenile; maybe that was due to his size.

Wait till Honor Bawell meets him, Anke thought. *She'll find some reason to host a winter activity for the older singles in our* g'may *and the Serenity Ridge district.*

She'd undoubtedly ask Anke to go, too— and Anke would say no. It wasn't that she begrudged her unmarried friends an opportunity to enjoy a time of recreation and fellowship with each other. It was that their underlying motivation more often than not seemed to be that they wanted to find someone to court. Anke figured since she wasn't interested in having a suitor, it was better if she didn't participate. Not to mention, she was usually busy doing something with her family anyway.

"*Guder mariye*, Josiah," Anke said when Velda finished telling him all about Ernest's butcher shop.

"*Guder mariye*," he replied stiffly.

Am I just imagining it, or is he acting different than he did yesterday? she wondered. *Maybe he's annoyed because I'm late?* "Sorry to keep you waiting. I'll get my coat and then we can go." She handed the baby to Velda. After donning her wool coat, she twisted a scarf around her head and neck and then pulled on a pair of mittens.

"*Denki* for the *kaffi*." While Josiah placed his cup on the counter near the sink and then donned his hat, Millie pulled on Anke's arm.

Anke bent down and the girl cupped her hands over Anke's scarf by her ear. "Did you see his hair?" she asked in a loud whisper. "It looks just like a rooster's comb."

Hoping Josiah hadn't heard the little girl,

Anke swallowed a giggle and whispered back, "*Jah.* Isn't it *wunderbaar*? But it's not polite to tell secrets in front of other people, remember?"

Anke and Josiah had barely made it off the porch before he gruffly remarked, "It's not polite to keep secrets behind people's backs, either."

"Ach. I'm sorry—I didn't realize you could hear us." Anke was surprised by his sternness; didn't he take Millie's age into account? "We expect the *kinner* to mind their manners, but sometimes they forget. But I know what Millie said was intended to be a compliment."

"I don't mean *that*," he replied scornfully. "I'm referring to the secret you kept from me about why you really needed to move into the *daadi haus*."

Anke stopped walking. "But I—I told you why. I distinctly remember saying I needed a place to stay with my nephew while my *schweschder* was in a recovery program."

"You didn't say it was because she has a drinking problem. I thought she was *sick*."

"I'm sorry if I wasn't clear. I didn't deliberately try to deceive you—although, to be honest, I really don't believe my *familye*'s situation is any of your business."

to start off on the wrong foot with the majority of the community members. On the other hand, he really needed the money. More important, despite the fact that Anke had said she wouldn't hold him to his commitment, Josiah felt obligated to honor his word.

I suppose it won't take very long to fix the roof and do a few basic repairs inside to make the place livable, he decided. *Besides, Keith knows I didn't deliberately choose to go against the community's preference in this matter. As long as I keep my distance from Anke and her nephew socially, I shouldn't experience the same kind of treatment I received in Illinois.*

"Anke, wait!" he called as he bounded across the yard. When he caught up to her, he said, "I still want the job."

She nodded, but didn't say anything else. They continued until they reached the *daadi haus*, but when she started up the porch stairs, Josiah warned, "Don't step there!" The board was so rotted it might have given way beneath her. If the condition of the porch was this poor, he could only imagine what the inside of the house was like.

A second later, Anke pushed open the door and Josiah had his answer: devoid of furniture, the interior was thickly coated with dust and he immediately noticed mice droppings on the windowsills, many of which were as rotten and chipped as the porch steps.

"Stay here by the door," he advised her. "I want to make sure this place isn't going to *kumme* crashing down on our heads before you go any farther."

She giggled, as if she thought he was joking, but he was serious. The *daadi haus* was so small, it only contained four rooms. The front door opened into the small living room on the left side of the house; behind it was the kitchen. On the right side were two tiny bedrooms, with a bathroom in between them. It didn't take Josiah long to make his assessment.

"The *gut* news is that the woodstove seems to be in working order," he said. "And there's no issue with the plumbing, either. But the leak has affected both bedrooms and I'm going to need to take out part of the wall to check for mold, as well as replace some floorboards and window frames. I can patch up the roof by *Muundaag* well enough to get you through the winter. But you're not going to be able to sleep in the bedrooms until the following week, at least."

Anke twisted her mouth to one side, and nodded slowly. "Okay, then we'll just have to sleep in the living room. It'll be warmer by the woodstove anyway."

"I doubt two beds will fit in here."

"Oh, we don't have beds. I intend to borrow a couple of cots. And if no one has any to spare, I'll put extra blankets down for padding and Will and I will bundle up in quilts. We'll be fine once I give this place a *gut* cleaning," she said cheerfully. "Now *kumme* with me to the barn—I'll show you the wood and supplies my *bruder* said you can use."

As Josiah stepped out of the drab, dilapidated little dwelling, he thought, *If she's willing to live in there for over a month in this weather, taking care of her nephew must be really important to her.* By the same token, if her family was forcing her to stay in this *daadi haus* with a child, they must have been adamantly opposed to inviting the boy into their house with them.

It's understandable they'd both have strong feelings about the matter, Josiah thought. But, as Anke had pointed out, her family's situation was none of his business. His only task was to make the tiny house livable again—and that was going to be a big enough challenge.

By late Friday afternoon, Josiah was nearly done repairing the roof. It hadn't been easy;

the temperatures were well below freezing and the windchill factor was even lower than that. But he couldn't wear gloves because they'd interfered with his ability to hold nails in place. So it was just easier to go bare-handed. It was also slower, because every couple of minutes he kept having to stop and blow on his fingers to warm them.

Also, he'd had to make several trips to the hardware store. Although he'd been able to use some of Ernest's tools, lumber and supplies, he had needed to purchase an equal amount of materials brand-new.

Additionally, there were interruptions from Anke, who seemed to constantly be asking him if he wanted more coffee or something to eat. While he appreciated her consideration, he was concerned if he accepted her offers, she'd take a break with him, too. He was here to work and he didn't want to give Anke the impression he was interested in socializing.

Nor did he want her sister-in-law—who seemed to spend an inordinate amount of time shaking out rugs on the porch—to glance over and see him and Anke standing beside the *daadi haus* eating muffins and drinking coffee together. If she did, Velda might have concluded Josiah was friendlier with Anke than he really was. Or even that he sided with her in regard to the issue of bringing an *Englisch* child into their family and *g'may*. So he always turned down Anke's offers of treats and drinks, even when his stomach was rumbling and it would have warmed his fingers to wrap them around a mug of hot coffee.

Sometimes when he was up on the roof, he could hear Anke singing indoors below him as she scrubbed the floors or washed the windows. He couldn't hear the words, but he could tell by the tune how joyful she was.

I don't understand how she can be so hallich, *knowing that the* leit *are judging her for what she's about to do,* he thought. *If I had a choice, I never would have willingly gone through what I experienced in Illinois. Yet it doesn't seem to make any difference to her.*

Josiah shifted his position on the steep incline and a couple of loose shingles slid over the edge to the ground below. *What this place really needs is metal roofing,* he thought. *It's more durable and it would keep the* haus *a lot warmer.* But he supposed since Anke only intended to stay in it for a month and a half, it wasn't worth the investment.

He descended the ladder and even before he'd reached the bottom, he heard the children's voices nearby and his heart skipped a beat. He had asked Velda to be sure to announce her arrival if she came in the area with the kids. What if one of the falling shingles had landed on them? By the time he got down, they had gone inside.

"Wilkom," Velda greeted him when he opened the door, as if she was the queen of the castle. *"Kumme* in quickly—you're letting the heat out and this place is already too drafty as it is."

"Hello, *kinner.*" He tugged on Millie's hat and gave Micah a playful nudge before turning to their mother. "Hello, Velda. You know, you really should be more careful bringing them here," he warned her. "It's not safe—"

Velda's eyebrows shot up and she didn't allow him to finish his sentence. "It's not safe for Anke to live here with Will?"

Josiah could hear the eager hope in her voice. *"Neh.* I was going to say it isn't safe for you to bring the *kinner* here without announcing your presence. I try to keep an eye out for anyone entering the area, but I didn't hear you *kumme* over. A couple of shingles slid off the roof—they could have hit one of you on the head."

"Sorry, I forgot," Velda blithely apologized. "The *kinner* were so excited about seeing where Will and Anke will be staying. Although we can't see all that much—it's awfully dark in here, isn't it?"

"That's because it's a dreary day," Anke explained. "But once the sun comes out again, or when I get a lamp in here, it'll be brighter."

"A kerosene lamp? Won't that be dangerous with a small *bu* in the *haus*? Especially an *Englischer* who isn't used to them? You know how curious some *kind* can be about fire." For some reason, Velda's tone sounded more critical than concerned.

"I wasn't planning to use a kerosene lamp—"

"Well, don't get any ideas about using our propane lamps," Velda interrupted. She seemed to do that quite often. "*We* need them."

Most of the Old Order Amish people Josiah knew didn't use kerosene lamps, either. They utilized gas-powered lights that were built into their walls. Or else they used a different kind of propane lamp; it was attached to a rolling stand that also contained a cabinet where the tank was stored. The entire contraption could be wheeled from room to room. This was the kind of lamp Velda said she couldn't spare for Anke's use.

Josiah noticed that she seemed stingier than her husband when it came to helping Anke prepare the *daadi haus* for Will's arrival. He wondered if she was normally so closefisted or if withholding something Anke needed was Velda's way of expressing disapproval. In this case, Velda's refusal to allow her sister-in-law to use the lamp might have been for the best anyway; using a propane tank in such a small, enclosed area didn't seem like the safest idea.

Apparently, it made Anke nervous, too, because she said, "I had no intention of using a propane lamp in here. I'm going to buy a battery-operated one."

Velda clicked her tongue against her teeth. "My, my. Between paying Josiah to work and all the things you'll need to buy to make this place inhabitable, I'm concerned that the expenses are really adding up."

"It won't cost you a penny, so the worry's all mine," Anke said. She smiled sweetly, but Josiah knew full well what she meant; she was politely indicating her sister-in-law should mind her own business in regard to how Anke spent her money.

Quite honestly, Josiah kind of felt that way about Velda himself. *Why did she bring up the topic of my salary?* It was insulting: almost as if she thought he shouldn't be paid. Granted, if he'd been at a work frolic, he wouldn't have received compensation. But this wasn't a frolic—it was his livelihood.

Before he knew it, he heard himself saying, "My *bruder* has an extra battery-operated lamp you can borrow while he's away, Anke." As soon as the words were out of his mouth, Josiah regretted them. Would Velda tell the others he was going out of his way to help Anke host her nephew?

"Will can use my flashlight so he can find his way to the bathroom in the dark," Asher volunteered. "Or if he wants to look at a book beneath his covers like I do sometimes."

"Denki," Anke replied, grinning at both of them. Then she turned to the twins and asked, "What do you think of this *daadi haus*?"

"I like it," Millie said. "But where are you going to sit?"

"I'm going to bring the folding table and chairs over from the barn."

"I can help you," Asher offered.

"Me, too!" echoed Micah.

"That table's too heavy for you *buwe* to carry," Velda informed them. *"Kumme.* Let's go back to the house and have some hot chocolate."

After the door closed behind them, Anke turned to Josiah, her expression shining. "That's very kind of you to allow me to use your *bruder's* lamp. *Denki.*"

"Don't mention it. As I said, he has a spare," he said, shrugging off her appreciation so she'd understand he wasn't showing her any preferential treatment. Since he needed to go buy groceries and run a couple of other errands, he told her he'd finished the roof so he was going to leave for the day. "What time is Will coming on *Muundaag*?"

"Around three o'clock, I believe."

"*Gut.* I'll have plenty of time to rehang the front door on *Muundaag* morning." Josiah had noticed it was hanging crooked, so it was letting in a draft. By rehanging the door, he'd create a better seal and the *daadi haus* would feel at least a degree or two warmer.

"Aren't you coming tomorrow, too? It would be *wunderbaar* if you could get a start on the bedrooms. As you mentioned, it's going to be tight quarters for us in here."

"*Neh.* I can't. I'm attending a work frolic tomorrow." Keith had told him about it during one of Josiah's return trips to the hardware store. "I think almost all of the young *menner* from New Hope will be there."

Anke appeared surprised. "*Jah*, they will be. But it doesn't take that many *menner* to raise a workshop—you're the only person who's repairing my *daadi haus*. One day could make a big difference to me, but they probably wouldn't even notice if you're not at the frolic."

Actually, I think they would. But even if they

don't, I'm not going to risk it, Josiah thought. "I didn't realize you expected me to work on *Samschdaag*, so I already told them I was coming. I can't change my plans now. It wouldn't be right."

I certainly can't fault him for wanting to keep his word, Anke thought after Josiah left. *And since he's new in town, the frolic will be a* gut *opportunity for him to get acquainted with some of the other* menner *in our district.*

Yet she was still disappointed that he wasn't going to make more progress on the *daadi haus* before Monday. As she'd pointed out, Omer Wilford already had plenty of men—including Anke's own brother—who would help him raise his workshop on Saturday, but she had no one except for Josiah. And now she didn't even have him.

It wasn't for a lack of trying. She had asked Ernest to put out the word that she needed additional help. She'd hoped that some of the older men who weren't assisting Omer might be able to pitch in on the *daadi haus* repairs on Saturday, but they'd all claimed they couldn't. Anke didn't doubt they were busy, but she had the feeling they would have made time to help her if it wasn't for the fact that she was taking in an *Englisch* child.

After all, her sister-in-law wasn't the only person in their district who'd been very outspoken about the decision Anke had made. Just this week while she was out running errands, she'd been stopped on four different occasions by people from her *g'may* who questioned whether she was really doing the right thing by taking care of Will.

Her answer was always the same—"I've prayed about it and it's not a violation of the *Ordnung,* so I believe it's what the Lord would have me do."

But as she looked around the shabby little *daadi haus,* she had her doubts. *Velda's right. It's too dark in here. And there's no furniture.* The folding table and chairs would be fine for mealtimes, but where were they going to sit to relax?

I might as well bring in some bales of hay to use as armchairs, Anke thought ruefully, fighting back the tears. *Despite all the money it's costing me to have this* haus *repaired, it's really not much better than a stable.*

Her intention was to provide a healthy, loving home for Will, but she hadn't fully considered how the boy might feel to live in such a rickety little building. Furthermore, how would Velda's attitude affect him? Anke didn't want Will to feel as if he was less precious in *Gott*'s sight—or in hers—than any of her other nieces and nephews were. But how could he not feel that way if he was rejected by most of his family?

For the first time since she'd made up her mind that she'd watch Will, Anke wondered if she was making a big mistake. So she dropped to her knees and prayed aloud.

"Dear *Gott*, if I'm wrong to keep Will here, please make that very plain to me. It would be very painful to release him into foster care, but if that's what's best for him, please allow it to happen." She stopped praying to dry her cheeks with her apron and then she added, "But if it's best for him to stay here, please protect him from hurtful attitudes. And help us reflect Your grace to Will, and to each other."

As she rose to her feet, Anke noticed a little patch of sunlight dancing on the floor. It was as if the Lord was reminding her He was the source of all the light and love the little home needed, and it made her feel like dancing, too.

Chapter Three

On Sunday, Anke bustled about in the basement kitchen, helping the other women prepare platters of bread, bologna, cheese, Amish peanut butter, egg salad, pretzels, beets, pickles and an assortment of cookies for the after-church meal. Unlike in most Amish districts in the country, some of the Amish communities in Maine, including the one in New Hope, met every other week in a church building instead of taking turns hosting worship in their homes. The central location was one of the advantages of the church and its large, spacious kitchen was another.

"Anke, is it true that Clara is abandoning her *bobbel* with you because she has a drinking problem?" Faith Smoker asked nonchalantly as she filled a pitcher with water. Almost instantly, a hush fell over the room and the other women continued performing their tasks in silence.

Anke would have preferred to keep the particular details of Clara's situation private within her family, but since that had been impossible from the start she figured it was best to set the record straight honestly and matter-of-factly. "That's not exactly accurate," she clarified. "But *jah*, as you've apparently heard, I did meet with Clara recently and she told me she gave birth to a *bu*, Will, out of wedlock five years ago during her *rumspringa*."

"For shame," one of the older women exclaimed and someone else clicked her tongue. Apparently, this was the first time the two of them had heard the news about Clara, but no one else seemed surprised.

"*Jah*, it is a shame. It was very upsetting to learn about the kind of life Clara has been living since she left New Hope and our *familye*. Especially because we've been praying faithfully for her," Anke acknowledged openly, her face growing hot. As she sliced a loaf of homemade wheat bread, she didn't look up, but she could feel the other women's eyes on her. Although she felt disgraced by her sister's story, she repeated it as straightforwardly as she could, ending, "So that's why Will is coming to stay with us for six weeks."

"Not with *us*," Velda clarified when she entered the kitchen just as her sister-in-law finished speaking. "He's staying with Anke in the *daadi haus*."

"In the *daadi haus*?" Arleta Lehman repeated incredulously. "Is that what Iddo said the *Ordnung* requires?"

Iddo Stoll was New Hope's deacon. After Ernest and Velda agreed that Will could stay with Anke in the *daadi haus*, Ernest had discussed the situation with Iddo, too, because Velda wanted to be sure they weren't violating any ordinances. "*Neh*. Iddo told my *bruder* it would have been permissible for Will to visit our *familye* on a temporary basis in our home," Anke answered.

"But I think most of the *mamms* here can understand why I don't want Will to live in the same *haus* with my *kinner*. I'm worried about his influence on them," Velda asserted and several of the other mothers of young children indicated they agreed with her concerns.

Anke understood why it was so important that they protect their families from the *Englisch* influence, but she hoped this didn't mean they wouldn't allow their young children to play with Will at all. She assured them, "I'm going to do my best to see to it that my nephew behaves himself and abides by our customs while he's staying with us—with *me*, I mean."

"Of course, you will. Although he's bound to misbehave from time to time, just as all our *kinner* do." Arleta gave Anke a sympathetic smile. "I'm sorry to hear about your sister's situation, but it must have been such a blessing for you to see her again? And to know that as long as she's alive, there's still hope for *Gott* to change her heart."

Anke was almost moved to tears by Arleta's empathy. The young mother of a young daughter seemed to understand what it had meant to Anke to see her sister again—and to focus on God's redeeming power, instead of on Clara's wrongdoings. "*Denki* for asking. You're right—I was overjoyed when Clara reached out to me. Even though I regret the circumstances, I'm *hallich* that I get to care for her *suh*."

"But how will you stay in the *daadi haus*? Is it even habitable?"

"Not yet, but it will be by *Muundaag.* Victor's *bruder* Josiah has been repairing it. He just moved to New Hope from Illinois."

"So *that's* who that *mann* was sitting over by the window," Honor Bawell blurted out, snapping her fingers.

Several women chuckled at her blatant curiosity about New Hope's newest bachelor and then they resumed their separate conversations with each other. Relieved she was no longer the center of their attention, Anke began chatting with Honor, who said a group of singles was going snowshoeing together that afternoon.

"It's going to be a lot of *schpass*," she said. "Faith, Jacob, Keith, Glenda and Ervin are all going. I should invite Josiah, too. His *bruder* must have snowshoes he can borrow. Would you like to *kumme*?"

"I can't. I told Velda I'd watch the *kinner* so she and Ernest can take a nap. Charity is teething so neither of them has gotten much sleep lately."

"Oh, that's too bad. It seems like you hardly ever get to socialize with us single people." Honor stacked a plate high with the bread Anke had been slicing and set it on a tray. "So, tell me, what's Josiah like?"

Anke chuckled, realizing that Honor was already trying to determine if he'd be someone she'd consider as a suitor. "I'll let you decide that for yourself after you meet him."

"Just tell me a little bit," Honor wheedled. "Like if he's quiet or talkative? Serious? Funny?"

Anke certainly wouldn't describe him as talkative. She'd tried to be cordial, but he hadn't accepted any of her offers of coffee or sweets. He seemed rather standoffish and she was inclined to think he wasn't very personable, except he always gave Velda's children a warm hello and sometimes he'd playfully tease them. And he volunteered to allow her to use Victor's lamp, which was considerate of him. Still, Anke didn't have a strong sense of his character, so she simply told Honor, "He's been too busy working on the *daadi haus* for me to chat with him. All I really know is that he's a *gut* carpenter. Very thorough." *He's also very strong and he has the prettiest hair I've ever seen on a* mann, Anke thought. But it would have been an inappropriate remark for her to make. Besides, Honor could see that for herself.

"Humph." Honor made a dissatisfied sound and muttered, "If I didn't know better, I'd think you're deliberately being evasive because you're interested in a courtship with him yourself or something."

"Believe me, I'm not," Anke replied with a chuckle. Not that she'd tell Honor if she *was* interested in having Josiah as a suitor, but that was beside the point. "I appreciate his work on the *daadi haus*, but right now my sole focus is on preparing a place for my nephew to stay with me."

"All right, but I hope you don't regret it if Josiah winds up courting someone else," Honor warned.

"As I said, courting is the last thing on my mind," Anke reiterated. "But I'm *hallich* to introduce you to Josiah after lunch, if you'd like me to."

"That would be *wunderbaar.*" Honor beamed, obviously as determined to enter into a courtship as Anke was to avoid one.

Josiah pushed his hat farther down on his head as he stepped out of the church and crossed the yard. He had almost reached the hitching post when he heard a woman call his name. Turning, he spotted Anke and another woman approaching him. Even before Anke introduced him to the tall, smiling, dark-haired woman, Josiah guessed she was Honor Bawell, the one Victor had told him about.

She welcomed him to New Hope and then invited Josiah to go snowshoeing with a group of young men and women from the district. When she listed their names, he noticed she didn't mention Anke's. "We're going on the trails in the woods by the gorge. It's beautiful there and the conditions should be perfect because of last night's snowfall," she told him, gesturing toward the pristinely white field in the distance.

Among the Amish, Sunday was traditionally considered a day for socializing as much as it was considered a day of rest. But after the incident at the golf course, Josiah had grown so accustomed to keeping to himself on the Sabbath that he'd gotten used to being alone. Also, after a week that included making a long trip, working on the *daadi haus* during the day and his brother's kitchen floor during the evening, as well as attending a work frolic, he was worn-out. He'd been looking forward to stopping at the phone shanty to call his family. Afterward, he intended to go home and relax with a cup of hot cocoa as he read Scripture or one of the books about Maine that he'd found on his brother's shelf. So he declined, saying, "*Denki*, but I don't have snowshoes."

"Doesn't your *bruder* have a pair you can use?" Honor pressed him.

"I—I'm not sure—I haven't looked around for any. But even if he does, I've never gone snowshoeing before. I should get some practice, first, so I don't slow everyone else down."

"You don't have to worry about that—I'm not very fast, either." Honor peered at him from beneath her lashes. "You and I can keep each other company if we lag behind the others."

It dawned on Josiah that maybe she wasn't

the community matchmaker after all; maybe she was looking for a suitor for *herself.* Or was she just being friendly? He couldn't tell, but either way, he didn't want to do anything that might result in the two of them spending time alone together. "I appreciate the offer, but I've had a long week and I was planning to go call my *familye* and then relax for the afternoon."

As he was speaking, Keith came up to where the trio was standing and echoed Honor's sentiments. "You definitely should *kumme* with us, Josiah. The way the weather changes around here, you might not get another opportunity like this again until next year."

Before Josiah could refuse for a fourth time, Anke, who had been quietly shifting from foot to foot and rubbing her arms as if she was cold, spoke up. "Quit pressuring him, you two! The poor *mann* just traveled halfway across the country. He probably needs a little time to adjust to being here before he goes mountain climbing on the coldest day of the year with you."

Anke's tone was lighthearted and she was clearly exaggerating so they'd let Josiah off the hook. He shot her a grateful look and she acknowledged it with a discreet little smile and nod of her head.

Josiah was about to remark that she was

right, but Keith cut in. There was an edge to his voice as he needled her, asking, "What's the matter, Anke? Are you worried he'll fall and injure himself and then he won't be able to repair the *daadi haus* for you?"

Anke's mouth fell open and she took a step back before replying, "*Neh*, of course not. If Josiah—or anyone else—injured himself, I'd be far more concerned about his well-being than about the *daadi haus*." The ribbon of Anke's winter church bonnet blew across her cheek and as she smoothed it down, Josiah noticed the hurt look in her sea-green eyes. Backing farther away from the group, she said, "My *familye* must be wondering what's keeping me, so I'd better go. Have *schpass* snow-shoeing, everyone."

As she walked out of earshot, Keith mumbled, "She's awfully defensive about the *daadi haus*—that's the sign of a guilty conscience."

Josiah had actually found Keith's comment to Anke to be unsettling, too. It was understandable if he disagreed with her plans to care for her *Englisch* nephew, but why had he brought it up when they'd all been talking about a completely different subject? It was almost as if he was antagonizing her, which would have been unkind. *Maybe he was try-*

ing to be funny, Josiah thought, trying to give him the benefit of the doubt.

Instead of acknowledging Keith's remark, he said to Honor, "*Denki* again for the invitation, but as I said, I'm going to relax at home this afternoon. I'll look around the *haus* and barn to see if Victor has any snowshoes. If he does, I'll be able to join you the next time you go."

"*Gut.*" Honor batted her lashes at him. "We'll hold you to that—no excuses if you're tired or the weather's bad."

"Don't worry. No matter how unpleasant the circumstances, Josiah always keeps his word, don't you?" Keith asked.

Puzzled by what he meant, as well as by the sarcasm in his voice, Josiah answered, "With *Gott*'s help, I try."

It wasn't until he'd walked away that Josiah caught on—Keith had been alluding to the fact that Josiah was honoring his word to repair Anke's *daadi haus*, even if it wasn't for an ideal purpose. It was the second time Keith had brought up the topic out of the blue, so it must have really been troubling him. *How many other people in New Hope feel as strongly about Anke's decision as Keith does*? he wondered. No one had mentioned anything about it at the frolic. But then again, no one had done much talking at all—they were too busy racing to raise the workshop before it began to snow. So Josiah couldn't make any assumptions about their opinions on the matter.

I wish I'd never taken the job, he thought as he unhitched his brother's horse from the post. *Fortunately, it won't be long until I'm finished with it and then I won't have to worry about whether or not people are judging me as being guilty by association.*

On Monday morning, Anke was so nervous and excited she could hardly eat anything for breakfast. However, pudgy little Charity leaned forward in her high chair as far as she could, reaching for the untouched slice of French toast on Anke's plate.

"*Neh—neh,* you little *schnickelfritz.*" Anke laughed as she pushed the dish out of reach. "You've had enough bread and syrup. Here, try a little bit of scrambled egg."

"Are there this many days until Will gets here?" Millie asked, holding up her index finger.

"*Neh.* He's coming today, so there are zero more full days left. Like this." Anke curled her fingers into a circle and then peered through them, making Millie giggle. She loved how joyful her nieces and nephews were about Will coming to New Hope.

"He's coming at three o'clock. That's after lunch but before supper," Asher said, repeating to his younger siblings what Anke had told him the night before. "You two might still be napping."

"I don't want to still be napping. I want my eyes to be wide-open so I can see him," Micah objected.

Millie nearly tipped her glass of milk over as she set it on the table and announced, "I want my eyes to be wide-open when Will *kummes*, too."

"You'll all get a chance to see your *gschwischderkind*, but not until your *ant* shows him where he's going to live. He needs to get settled into the *daadi haus*, first." Velda had taken every opportunity to remind her children that Will was only allowed into the main house at her invitation. So Anke was amazed when her sister-in-law added, "Your *daed* and I decided last night that Will and Anke should have supper here in the *haus* with us today. You can meet him then."

Anke suspected her brother was the one who'd made the decision a long time ago. He'd probably been trying to convince Velda all week that it was the hospitable thing to do. Regardless of how the decision came about,

Anke couldn't have been any happier and the children were thrilled, too. They spontaneously erupted in a collective cheer.

"That's a *wunderbaar* invitation, Velda. *Denki*," Anke said.

"Don't get used to it," Velda warned them all sternly. "It's just this one time, in celebration of Valentine's Day."

In New Hope, the Amish usually marked the holiday with homemade cards and special desserts. But because she'd been so focused on preparing the *daadi haus* for Will's arrival, Anke had completely forgotten today was Valentine's Day. "Oh, *neh*!" she exclaimed. "I just remembered that I have to deliver the special-order apron I made to Millers' Restaurant by noon."

The eatery was too far away for her to walk to it and Ernest had taken the buggy to his butcher shop, which was three miles across town. In warmer weather, Anke could have made the trek, but today there was a stiff wind and she still had so many things to get done before Will arrived. *I can't risk upsetting a customer or I might lose business*, she fretted. *And I'm going to need the income now that I'll be buying extra food for Will and me.*

As much as she hated to impose on Josiah,

there was no way around it—Anke was going to have to ask if she could take his horse and buggy.

Josiah was surprised Anke hadn't come to the *daadi haus* yet; it was almost ten o'clock and usually she showed up by nine. He had to give her credit; by cleaning the walls, windows and floors, and by painting the cupboards, she had brightened the dingy kitchen and living room considerably.

But the lack of furniture kept the place from being very cozy. Right now, there were only a folding table and four chairs in the kitchen and a rocker in front of the woodstove in the living room. *Are they really going to sleep on cushions if no one has any cots or beds they can use*? he wondered. He'd rehung the front door, but he could feel a draft coming from one of the living room windows—and the bedroom windows were even draftier.

Ideally, most of the windows in the *daadi haus* should have been replaced. But since he knew Anke didn't have the time or money for him to do that, Josiah decided he'd talk to her about putting plastic wrap over them once he'd finished recaulking the frames. *I need to get more caulk at the hardware store*, he suddenly remembered. *I could pick up the plastic then.*

As he was dithering about whether to go into town now or wait until he'd talked to Anke about purchasing plastic wrap, she burst through the door with two cardboard boxes in hand. *"Guder mariye,"* they greeted each other as she carried the boxes into the kitchen. When she returned he noticed her forehead was puckered with lines and she was biting her lower lip. Was she dissatisfied with the work he was doing?

"I'm afraid I have to ask a favor," she began, before explaining that she needed to deliver an apron she'd made to Millers' Restaurant by noon. "Would you mind if I borrowed your *gaul* and buggy?"

Josiah hesitated, calculating how many miles Victor's horse would have to travel in the blustery weather if Anke went out and returned and then he made a second trip to the hardware store, as well as back home at the end of the day. He supposed he could offer to drop the apron off on his way to pick up the caulk, but he didn't know where the restaurant was. Besides, then he'd have to explain to the Millers why he was running Anke's errand. He didn't want to draw attention to the fact he was working on her *daadi haus*. Finally, he answered, "I have to go to the hardware store, so you can *kumme* with me and drop it off."

"*Denki*, Josiah," she exclaimed and dashed back to the house to get the apron while he went to the stable to hitch the horse and buggy.

Once they were underway, it occurred to him he should have asked if Velda and the children wanted to come with them, too. In his district in Illinois, it wasn't necessarily unusual for an Amish man and Amish woman who were single to share a daytime ride into town in a buggy and no one thought much of it. But Josiah was aware that in some Amish communities, people assumed it meant they were courting. He was so worried about it that he didn't realize Anke had asked him a question until he noticed her eyeing him. "I'm sorry. What did you say?"

"I asked whether Honor talked you into snowshoeing after all or if you were able to go home and get some rest."

"I went home." A moment passed and Josiah recognized he'd sounded cranky, so he asked, "Have you ever been snowshoeing with the group?"

"Once or twice. I enjoyed it, but I couldn't go yesterday because I was watching the *kinner* so Velda could rest."

"Oh. Is she ill?"

"*Neh*. But Charity is teething, so she hasn't been getting much sleep. Neither has my *bruder*

Ernest. I'm a little worried about how they'll fare without me around to help—ack! That sounds so boastful, doesn't it? I don't mean it like that. I just know how difficult it can be to care for four young *kinner* when you're overly tired. So for their sake, I hope Charity cuts those teeth soon."

You're the one who probably isn't going to be getting much sleep in the near future, Josiah thought. "At least you'll be right next door if your sister-in-law needs your help—or if you need hers."

"*Jah,* but since she's limiting how often I'm allowed to *kumme* to the *haus* with—" Anke stopped speaking midsentence and pointed out a potato farm owned by the Wittmer family. Then she rambled on about other Amish families who owned farms in their community. But Josiah wasn't fooled. He knew she was trying to distract him because she was embarrassed she'd let it slip that her sister-in-law was limiting her visits with her nephew to the main house.

He certainly understood why Velda wouldn't want her children living with or being influenced by an *Englischer.* But from what he understood, Anke was the owner of both houses on the property and she had voluntarily relinquished the main residence out of regard for her brother and sister-in-law's reservations about Will. So it seemed strange that Velda would feel she had the need or right to impose restrictions on Anke's visits, especially if her intention was to help care for Velda's children.

Josiah reminded himself that their family dynamics were none of his business and he began explaining his observation about the windows in the *daadi haus* to Anke. "It's going to be awfully cold sleeping on the floor, even if you have cushions," he said. "That's why I think it would be wise to put plastic wrap over the windows."

"*Neh*, you can't do that—it will block out the light. Besides, Arleta Lehman said she has two spare cots I can use, so we won't be on the floor after all. She's bringing them over this afternoon. Isn't that *wunderbaar*?"

Josiah didn't have to turn his head to see that Anke was smiling—he could hear it in her voice. *She's so excited about having cots to sleep on that she doesn't even seem to mind that they only have a rocker and a couple of uncomfortable folding chairs for sitting.* He might not have agreed with her decision to take Will in, but Josiah had to admire her grateful, upbeat attitude.

When they reached the Millers' Restaurant, Anke dashed inside to deliver the apron. He hoped when they got to town she'd wait for him in the buggy, just in case people saw them out together. But when they pulled into the parking lot, she said she had to run down the street to buy cocoa for a cake she was making that afternoon. Josiah went into the hardware store and quickly found the caulk he needed, but Keith was helping an *Englisch* customer load something into his car. While Josiah was waiting at the register, Anke came in and stood beside him, pink-cheeked from the wind.

"It's so cold I thought I'd warm up in here until you're ready to leave," she said blithely. Her eyes were sparkling and she gave him such a fetching smile that Josiah felt guilty for wishing she hadn't come into the store. He wasn't worried that Keith would think they were courting, but Josiah suspected he'd have something to say about them being together anyway.

He wasn't wrong. After Keith entered the store and greeted them, he cracked, "So, you're not letting Josiah out of your sight today, eh, Anke? Afraid he's going to walk off the job before he finishes repairing the *daadi haus*?"

His remark instantly drained the exuberance from Anke's features. Her mouth fell open and she blinked several times, but before she could respond, Josiah spoke up. "I believe Anke trusts that I wouldn't walk off a job I agreed to undertake. If anyone seems concerned about my work on the *daadi haus*, it's you, Keith." Realizing he sounded harsher than he'd intended, Josiah grinned and added, "Don't worry—I intend to complete what I started, which is *gut* for business, since I'll probably be back in here buying more supplies again."

Keith furrowed his brow, as if he wasn't quite sure how to take Josiah's comment. It had clearly disconcerted him, though, because he gave him the wrong change after he rang up Josiah's purchase. But he let the matter drop, said goodbye and quickly scurried off.

Josiah and Anke returned to the buggy and neither one of them spoke as they made their way back to her house. They were almost there when she said, "You're right, you know, Josiah. I *do* trust that you won't walk off this job without completing it. And that means a lot to me, especially because…because some people in the community don't agree with what I'm doing. But with the exception of Keith, I don't think anyone will give you a hard time about helping me. *I'm* the one who's hosting an *Englischer*, not you."

Josiah knew from experience that that didn't necessarily mean he was in the clear. He also thought, *I'm not exactly sure that I agree with what you're doing, either.* But when he glanced sideways and caught sight of Anke fretfully studying him, he said the one positive thing he *did* know for sure. "I think it was *Gott*'s timing that you needed a carpenter and I needed a job."

"*Jah.* Otherwise, Will and I might have had to sleep in the barn," she said with an effervescent giggle that again indicated how good-natured she was being.

Something tells me that still wouldn't have stopped you from taking him in, Josiah thought and he grinned at her before turning his attention back to the road.

Chapter Four

Anke was beside herself with anticipation and nervousness as she paced the gravelly stretch of lane near the end of the driveway. In deference to Velda's concerns, she had agreed to meet Yolanda and Will out of sight from the main house—her sister-in-law hadn't wanted them to see their cousin arrive in a car. Her request didn't make much sense to Anke, since the children already knew he was *Englisch*. Furthermore, Ernest occasionally received a ride in a car from one of the *Englischers* who took him to various fairgrounds where he sold sausages. But Anke was determined not to give Velda any reason to complain that she wasn't being respectful of her wishes. So, she walked back and forth near the road, stamping her feet to keep her toes from going numb.

It must be closer to four o'clock than to three

by now. What could be keeping Yolanda? she wondered, hoping it wasn't that Clara had changed her mind. A knot of anxiety tightened in her stomach. *She wouldn't do that, would she?* Suddenly, Anke wished she had asked Josiah to stop at the phone shanty so she could have checked if she had any messages. Her fear that Will might not be coming after all made her stomach cramp and she stopped walking to clutch the fence post.

Please, Lord, bring Will to me soon, she silently prayed. She knew she should also ask for God to give her the grace to accept it if Clara had changed her mind, but Anke couldn't bear the thought. Not after all she'd done to prepare for Will's arrival. And not after harboring so much hope in her heart that her sister was on her way to changing her life around.

Her anxiety subsided and when she heard a car pulling up, she opened her eyes. Yolanda waved to her from behind the steering wheel. Before Anke reached the vehicle, Clara's sponsor had opened her door and stepped out. "Hello, Anke," she called. "Sorry to keep you waiting—my GPS kept rerouting me. Apparently it doesn't recognize this lane as a street."

"It's fine—I'm just glad you're here now."

Yolanda opened the passenger door behind her and a little boy hopped out. He was wearing a blue synthetic jacket and a blue knit hat with orange around the brim and an orange pom-pom on the top. Somewhere in the back of her mind, Anke registered the bright color, which was considered so flashy that some of the Amish men in New Hope had petitioned the state to allow them to wear yellow vests while they were hunting deer, instead of orange. *His hat will be the first thing to upset Velda*, she thought. But Anke's only concern at the moment was drawing near enough to see her nephew's face.

When she did, it took her breath away: he looked almost exactly like Clara had at that age—wide-set blue eyes, wispy blondish hair and an upturned nose. But unlike his mother, Will was slight—even though he was almost Asher's age, he appeared to be Micah's height and weight. His smallness made him seem especially vulnerable and Anke had to refrain from overwhelming him by gathering him into her arms.

"Will, this is your aunt Anke," Yolanda said. "She's going to take really good care of you until your mom is out of the hospital."

"Hello, Will. I'm very happy you're here with me." Anke spoke in *Englisch* and stepped closer. The little boy peered up at her.

"Are you Mommy's big sister? The one who pushed her really high on a swing?"

Anke was caught off guard, moved by the childhood memory Clara must have told him. "Yes, that's right, I am. I can show you the swing and all the other places where your mom used to play when she was a little girl."

Instead of replying, Will ducked into the back seat again and for a second, Anke's heart sank, thinking he wanted to leave. But then he pulled out a green backpack and adjusted it over his shoulders. "Can I go sledding on the really fast hill, too?"

Anke smiled. "*Jah*, once the weather gets a little warmer." She had noticed he was wearing sneakers instead of boots and his synthetic coat didn't appear very thick.

"It sounds like you're going to have a lot of fun here, Will," Yolanda remarked. She removed a small overnight bag from the trunk and handed it to Anke, along with her business card. "That's my cell phone number. I know it isn't easy for you to call, but if you need me for anything, don't hesitate to get in touch. I'll do the same if I…have any updates at all," she said discreetly.

After thanking her, Anke took Will's hand in hers. There wasn't any traffic and she wasn't worried he would slip, but she wanted him to feel a connection to her. Anke expected he might be shy at first since they'd never met and he was in an entirely new location, but he peppered her with questions as they tramped down the long driveway.

"Is this a farm?" he asked, pointing to the big yard.

"*Neh.* But we do grow vegetables for our family to eat in the spring and summer. And we have chickens and a horse and two milk cows."

"Can I pet them?"

"Yes, if an adult is with you and says it's all right. I can show you the animals tomorrow."

"What are their names?"

"We call the cows Brownie and Blondie. The horse's name is Star and you'll have to ask your *gschwischderkinner* what the chickens' names are because I can't remember them all."

Will stopped to bounce his book bag farther up on his back. "What's a *scwisher-kinner*?"

Anke hadn't realized she'd inserted an Amish word into her sentence. "*Gschwischderkinner* means cousins. You'll meet them later when we eat supper together."

"What are their names? Are they big like me?"

Anke smiled because he'd referred to himself as big and she told him his cousins' names and ages.

"Are they allowed to ride the horse?"

"No one here rides the horse, but he does pull the buggy and you can ride in that someday."

"Is it like the sleigh Santa rides in?"

Anke winced at the reference, but she didn't want to tell him there was no such person as Santa Claus and make him upset before they'd even reached the porch of the *daadi haus*. So she replied, "A buggy isn't open like a sleigh. It has a roof and walls and windows. You'll see one soon."

Anke hadn't realized quite how many Amish customs would be foreign to an *Englischer* Will's age. Hadn't Clara told him anything about their lifestyle? Even if she hadn't mentioned it to him while he was growing up, it seemed she should have told him this week, in preparation for his visit.

Suddenly, Will stopped cold and dropped Anke's hand. "Wow!" he exclaimed.

She immediately stopped, too, concerned he'd seen a moose along the edge of their property. Late afternoon or early evening was about the time of day when they were sometimes spotted in that part of Maine. "What is it?"

"That house is *huge*! Is that where I'm going to live?"

Anke's breath caught and for the briefest second, she had the impulse to tell him, *Yes. Yes, it is—just as soon as I tell my brother and sister-in-law I've changed my mind about staying in the* daddi haus.

"No. That's where your *gschwischderkinner* live. They have six people in their family, so they need more room than you and I do. You're going to live with me, over there." She pointed to the *daadi haus*.

"Wow!" he exclaimed again. "I never got to live in a log cabin before."

Anke's heart was ready to burst with delight over his reaction. *If living in a log cabin makes him that* hallich, *I'm not going to tell him it's called a* daadi haus, she thought as they continued toward it. When they reached the porch, she had to help him climb onto the first step because it was so high and his legs were so short. She could hear Josiah scraping the bedroom window inside and she paused before she opened the door. She hoped Will wasn't going to be disappointed when he saw the inside of his temporary home.

Arleta Lehman had brought over two folding cots shortly after Anke and Josiah returned from their trip to town this morning. So Anke had made up the narrow beds with the heaviest quilts she could find in the linen closet; fortunately, they had so many that Velda couldn't claim she couldn't spare them. Arleta had also given Anke an old armchair that had belonged to her husband's grandmother. She'd said she felt bad that the upholstery was threadbare in spots and that one of the springs poked out in the back, but Anke was very grateful to receive it. She figured it could be Will's chair and she'd take the rocker. In her estimation, they had all the furniture they needed, but Anke didn't know how an *Englisch* child, even one as poor as her sister's son, would feel about living in such a sparsely decorated house.

She turned the handle and pushed the door open, explaining, "Right now, we have to share this room until our bedroom walls and floors and windows are repaired. That's why there are beds in here."

"Me and mommy live in a studio 'partment, too," he knowingly informed her as he unzipped his jacket. "She lets me watch cartoons in bed."

"Hmm." Anke figured she'd better break the news to him sooner rather than later. "I'll let you read in bed, but you can't watch TV because we don't have one here."

"Why not? Did a bad guy steal it?"

"No…" Anke stalled, trying to recall the simple explanation she'd prepared in anticipation of questions like this. "You see, we're Amish. And Amish people don't live the same way other people do. We don't wear the same kinds of clothes or drive cars or use electricity or watch TV."

"Why not?"

By and large, the Amish didn't claim their lifestyle was the right way to live, nor did they claim theirs was the only true faith—doing so would have been considered prideful. So Anke chose her words carefully. "Well, because we believe that God wants us to be different from most of the world. He loves us so, so, so much and He wants us to love Him back—and to love other people, too. But if we're distracted by worldly…by the things a lot of other people do, sometimes we forget to focus on God and on our neighbors. Or sometimes we're tempted to do bad things God wouldn't want us to do."

"Does God think it's bad to watch cartoons?"

Anke had expected Will would have questions about the Amish lifestyle, but she wasn't expecting the boy to be quite so inquisitive. If she had been speaking to an *Englisch* adult, she would have replied that she didn't know the mind of God; she only knew and acted on her own beliefs. But how was she going to put that into an explanation a child could understand?

Having overheard much of Anke and Will's conversation, Josiah recognized what a spot she was in. He'd been waiting for the right moment to introduce himself, because he didn't want to interrupt them. But now it seemed an interruption might be welcome, so he put down his caulking scraper, opened the bedroom door and stepped into the living room. "Hello," he said affably to Anke and the small blond boy she was crouching down beside. There was a look of relief in her eyes as she stood up.

"Hello, Josiah. I'd like you to meet my nephew Will." She put her hand on the boy's shoulder. "Will, this is Josiah."

Will craned his neck to look up at him. "Hi… Are you Aunt Anke's boyfriend?" he asked.

Josiah was startled by the question, but he realized in the *Englisch* world, it wasn't considered unusual, even for a small child, to ask something like that. And he knew Will was probably just trying to get a sense of who was who in his new surroundings.

Anke seemed startled, too. "No, he's not. I don't have a boyfriend," she blurted out, confirming Josiah's hunch that she wasn't courting anyone. Then she added, "Adults here don't discuss things like that with children, Will. But Josiah is a carpenter. He's fixing the bedrooms so we can sleep in them."

"What happened to them?"

"A big branch fell on the roof, so then it had a leak. Some of the water warped the floor. And some of the wood around the windows is rotting out. I need to fix everything to make it nice and safe and warm for you and your *ant*."

"Did it rain on your head when there was a leak?" Will asked Anke, causing Josiah to realize the boy had thought Anke had always lived in the little house.

She probably didn't tell him she had to move into it because she didn't want him to know they've been banished from the main house, he thought. Catching her eye, he mouthed, "Sorry."

Anke gave him a small shrug and then looked down at Will. "*Neh.* I wasn't here when the tree fell onto the roof. No one has lived in this house for a long time. I usually live in the other house, but remember that I told you it's kind of crowded? So Josiah is fixing this house for us so we have room to stretch our arms and legs."

"Thanks, Mr. Josiah," Will said so gratefully it made Josiah feel guilty that he'd ever had second thoughts about working on the *daadi haus*.

"You're *wilkom*. But you don't have to call me mister," he told him. In most Amish communities, children didn't use titles to address their elders the way *Englisch* children did. "You can just call me Josiah."

"Okay," he agreed. "You can call me Will. But not Bill or Billy. That's what my mommy calls my daddy and it makes her very sad."

Josiah felt a mix of compassion and discomfort. On one hand, it was painful to imagine what kind of family life Will must have had. On the other, the child didn't seem to have any understanding about what was appropriate to disclose to a stranger and what wasn't. Granted, most children revealed information that was embarrassing to their parents from time to time. But for the child's sake—and for Anke's, too—Josiah hoped Will wouldn't be this forthcoming about his home life with everyone else in the district. *Anke's sure got her work cut out for her training Will how to conduct himself*, he thought.

She was holding her chin, as if trying to decide what to do next. Figuring she might want to speak with Will in private, Josiah excused himself to the barn. As he was sorting through the lumber Anke's brother said he could use,

Ernest returned from the butcher shop early and unhitched his horse and buggy. They chatted briefly and he helped Josiah find the kind of wood he needed. Then he invited him to stay for supper.

"I brought fresh meat home. We're having noodles and sausage," he said, reaching into his buggy and pulling out a thermal bag with one hand and a big pot of cyclamen with the other. "It's a Valentine's Day tradition in our *haus*—the flowers are Velda's favorite and noodles and sausage are mine."

Just the mention of the word *sausage* made Josiah's mouth water. Other than the cold church lunch, he hadn't had a homemade meal since he'd left Illinois. But did he really want to be with the Bachman family on Will's first night there?

Ernest seemed to read his mind. "I can understand your hesitation. It's been a…a tense situation and we've all had to make some difficult decisions. That's partly why I'd like you to join us for a special supper—because I appreciate that you're renovating the *daadi haus*. I would have liked to help, but I didn't have the time. And honestly, I've had to do what my wife and I thought was best for my *kinner*—just like Anke is doing what she believes is best for our nephew and *schweschder*."

Reading between the lines, Josiah could sympathize about what an untenable position Ernest must have been in. Essentially, he'd had to choose between his wife's and both of his sisters' preferences. "There's no need to explain. No need to thank me, either. Anke is paying me well to repair the *daadi haus*."

"Then *kumme* join us for supper just because there's nothing that hits the spot on a cold night quite like fresh pork sausage. If we're fortunate, the *weibsleit* will surprise us with a special dessert, too."

Josiah already knew that Anke had made a chocolate cake with buttercream frosting; the tantalizing aroma had filled the *daadi haus* all afternoon. "Sounds too *gut* to miss," he said to Ernest. "Count me in."

Ernest had carried Anke's dresser down from the house on Saturday when he returned from the frolic. She'd asked him to set it in the closet, so she and Will would have easy access to it. Her intention was to use the top two drawers and give him the bottom two. But when she helped him unpack his duffel bag, she realized he hardly had enough clothes to fill half of one of the drawers. *Is that because Clara knows most of his wardrobe wouldn't be appropriate in our community or is it because that's all he owns?* she wondered.

Glancing at his book bag, she said, "You can put the rest of your things in this drawer, here."

"Okay," he agreed and proceeded to shove the entire book bag into the bottom drawer.

"Don't you want to unpack it first?"

"Do I have to?"

Realizing that Will might have brought something from home he didn't want her to see yet, Anke didn't force the issue. "Well, I guess it's okay if we keep your book bag in the closet for now. You can unpack it later. Let's clean up and then you can help me with my surprise. But you have to keep it a secret."

"What is it?"

"You'll have to wait and see."

After they'd washed their hands and Anke had given Will a snack, she told him she needed help decorating the special cake she'd made for Valentine's Day. They frosted it together and then she allowed him to line heart-shaped pink candies around the circumference of the cake and some on top, as well.

"It looks perfect," she told him. "I think your cousins will like it."

"You mean my shwisher-kinner?"

"*Jah*, your *gschwischderkinner*," Anke replied, impressed that he was already trying to imitate her *Deitsch*. She had intended to introduce him to a few words each day, but maybe he'd be ready to learn more rapidly than that. It certainly would be to his advantage, since most young Amish children in New Hope primarily spoke *Deitsch*. Some, like her brother's children, understood conversational *Englisch*, but the majority only learned a few *Englisch* phrases here and there until they went to school. "Do you remember what I told you their names are?"

"Micah and Millie and… Charity and Ashes."

"Asher, *jah*. Your *onkel* is named Ernest and your *ant* is called Velda. They're all very happy to see you so I think it's time for us to walk up there," Anke suggested, setting the cake in a cardboard box she'd used that morning to carry utensils and a couple of pots and pans from the main house. She was half-tempted to suggest that Will leave his orange and blue hat at home and just zip his hood up instead. But she was more worried about his ears getting cold than she was about how her sister-in-law might react to the bright color.

Just as they were ready to walk out the door, Josiah walked in, carrying wood. To Anke's surprise and delight, he said Ernest had invited him for supper. *With Josiah there, everyone will be on their best behavior—and I don't necessarily mean the* kinner, she thought face-tiously. But in all seriousness, she appreciated the patient and diplomatic way Josiah had answered Will's many questions. His interactions with the boy had a calming effect on *her* and she felt like Josiah's presence during supper might make Velda feel more comfortable, too.

"I've got a few things to finish and then I'll *kumme* over a little before six," he said.

"No hurry. We're going early so Will can meet his *gschwischderkinner.*"

"That means my cousins," Will informed Josiah, as if he didn't know. He pointed at Josiah's head. "Is that a cowboy hat?"

"*Neh.* This is an Amish hat. It keeps my ears warm and the sun out of my eyes."

"I like it," Will remarked.

As they headed toward the main house, the wind whipped right through Anke's coat and Will crossed his arms against his chest. *He must be freezing*, she thought. Usually, Micah received Asher's hand-me-down clothes and shoes. If they were still usable by the time he outgrew them, Velda would pass them on to another boy in their district. But Anke hoped her sister-in-law still had a pair of boots or a coat that Will could use. A couple wool sweaters, too.

When they reached the house, she hesitated

on the porch and shifted the box in her arms. She almost felt as if she should knock to announce their arrival, yet something within her rebelled at the idea—it was still her home, after all. But as it turned out, Asher flung the door open from the inside.

"Hi, *Ant* Anke. Hi, Will," he said in *Englisch* and Millie and Micah copied him. Anke introduced them by name and when Velda came into the room carrying Charity, she introduced both of them, too.

"You *kinner* may play in the gathering room. I don't want you going upstairs," Velda cautioned her children in *Deitsch*. Then she instructed Will in *Englisch*, "When Amish men and boys come into the *haus*, they always take off their hats because that's the polite thing to do. They take off their shoes and boots at the door, too, so they don't track in snow and get the floors wet."

Ideally, jah. *But I've seen Micah and Asher wear their boots in bed while they've been taking a nap*, Anke thought defensively, but she held her tongue. In Amish communities, it was commonplace for adults to instruct and correct all children, not just their own offspring. Will would be expected to mind Velda, just as Velda and Ernest's children obeyed Anke. And if Anke had any qualms about Velda's instructions or vice versa, the women would address them in private, not in front of the children.

Will pulled off his sneakers, revealing a hole in the big toe of his left sock. Straightening up, he asked, "Can I keep my coat on? I'm cold."

"Coats are for outdoors, too," Velda said, but she softened her tone and added, "Asher, go bring Will a sweater from your bottom drawer. And another pair of socks, as well."

Asher charged down the hall just as Ernest came around the corner. When he saw Will, he stopped and did a double take. Anke knew why; it was because of Will's resemblance to Clara. But what surprised her was that Ernest's eyes welled—usually, it was more difficult to read his emotions. *This entire situation with Clara and Will must be troubling him more than I've realized*, she thought.

Ernest blinked and cleared his throat. "Hello, Will. I'm your uncle Ernest. I'm glad to see you," he said.

"Are you my mommy's brother? The one who runs faster than a black cow with big horns?"

Ernest chuckled. "Yes, one time when I was young, I made the mistake of crossing a field with a bull in it and he gave chase. I had to run really fast to make it back over the fence."

"Is a bull going to chase me across the field?"

"No. We don't have a bull here, just cows."

As Ernest reiterated the list of animals Anke had told Will they had on the property, she set the cardboard box down so she could remove her coat and go help Velda in the kitchen. Meanwhile, Asher bolted back down the hall with the sweater and socks for Will. When he'd put them on, the three children ushered him into the gathering room. Listening to their excited commotion, Anke beamed. *Denki, Lord, for helping Will's initial introduction to the familye go so smoothly*, she silently prayed. *Please continue to bless our time together.*

When Ernest opened the door, Josiah immediately noticed two things. The first was the sound of the children laughing. The second was the most delectable aroma he'd smelled since he'd left home in Illinois. His uneasiness about eating with the Bachmans immediately lifted.

He barely had time to wash his hands and say hello to the children before the women called everyone to come to the table. As they entered the kitchen, Anke greeted them with an enormous smile. Looking at her, Josiah suddenly remembered that during their teenage years, his mother occasionally told his sisters that nothing was more becoming on a young woman than a joyful heart. It was certainly true in Anke's case this evening; she was radiant with happiness. *I'm so glad everything seems to be going well*, Josiah thought, sitting in the chair Velda indicated was his.

"I hope everyone's *hungerich*, because we made a double batch of everything," Anke announced, practically singing.

"Even the special dessert?" Ernest teased.

"Dessert?" Anke feigned ignorance as she sat down across from Josiah. "Who told you we have dessert?"

Will looked worried. "*I* didn't tell him."

"*Neh*, he didn't," Ernest confirmed. "I guessed it because we always have a special dessert on Valentine's Day."

"There won't be dessert for anyone who doesn't eat their supper. So let's stop chattering and say grace," Velda admonished them.

Everyone bowed their heads, but as Ernest began to pray, Will asked, "Why is everybody hiding their eyes?"

"That's what we do when we thank God for our food," Anke whispered. "Shh."

Ernest began again in *Deitsch*, "*Gott—*"

Will piped up again. "Why doesn't God want us to see Him?"

"Shush," Velda scolded and clapped her hands together so sharply that even Josiah flinched.

He heard movement on the other side of the table, but Josiah didn't open his eyes until Ernest had completed his brief prayer. Then he realized that Will had slunk down beneath the table.

Anke was bending sideways in her chair, saying, "Will, come out from under there." The other children were absolutely silent, except for Charity, who was grunting as she leaned forward, trying to reach the plastic bowl of plain noodles her mother had set aside for her.

While Velda passed the serving dish to Josiah as if nothing had happened, Anke repeated, "Will, come out from under there."

"No," he refused, crying. "I don't want to. I want my mommy."

Velda leaned sideways to look under the table, too. "In this house, children do *not* tell their elders no," she barked. "If you don't behave, you won't be invited back."

"I'm handling this, Velda," Anke snapped, at which point Ernest pushed back his chair, got down on all fours and slid the boy out from beneath the table. He set him on his feet. Will's chin was dropped to his chest and his shoulders bounced up and down as he sobbed.

"Why don't you go with your Aunt Anke and she can get you a tissue," Ernest said quietly into his ear.

Anke took his hand and the pair left the room. Velda's face was scarlet, whether from the blood rushing to her head because she'd been tilting sideways or because she was upset. She continued passing the food around and serving it to the children. But Asher looked as if he was about to cry and Josiah had lost his appetite, too.

It's true that Will needs to learn gut *behavior and follow their household rules*, he thought. *But considering his age and that he's been separated from his* mamm *for the first time in his life, couldn't Velda have been little gentler about it?* Better yet, he thought she shouldn't have interfered at all, since Anke was already addressing the boy's behavior.

"Eat your noodles and sausage, Asher," Velda said.

"My *bauch* hurts."

"If your *bauch* hurts too much to eat supper, then it hurts too much to eat *kuche*, too."

Apparently, Asher's stomach really did hurt that much, because he nodded, but didn't pick up his fork. Josiah asked Ernest about how his business was doing, but he was too distracted by the muffled sound of Will sobbing in the gathering room to pay attention to his answer.

A few minutes later, Anke came back into the kitchen. "Will has had a long day and I think it's better if we eat alone this evening. I'm going to put some food in a container and we're going back to the *daadi haus*."

Velda pinched her lips together, but she didn't say anything as Anke moved about, filling a glass dish with enough noodles and sausage for her and Will. But when Velda noticed she had taken out a long knife, she objected, "You're not going to slice into the *kuche* before everyone has finished eating supper, are you?"

"Well, it's too cold outside for us to come back later to get our dessert, so *jah*, I am—unless you're willing to bring us two pieces when you're done?" When Velda didn't respond, Anke lifted the cake from the counter and brought it to the table. "Look, *kinner*. Before I cut it, I want you to see the special *kuche* your *gschwischderkind* helped me decorate for you and your *mamm* and *daed*—and for Josiah, too—for Valentine's Day."

Millie and Micah craned their necks and made awed sounds, but Asher said, "Can I be excused from the table so I can give the cards we made to *Ant* Anke and Will?"

Velda was chewing, so she held up a finger

indicating she'd answer in a moment, but before she could swallow, Ernest said, "*Jah*, go ahead, *suh*." As the boy quickly left the room, Josiah caught Velda scowling at her husband.

"*Gut nacht*, everyone," Anke said once she had cut and wrapped two pieces of cake for her and Will.

"*Gut nacht*," everyone except for Charity and Velda chorused.

"Happy Valentine's Day," Josiah added weakly, because nothing about the occasion felt happy anymore.

Chapter Five

❧

Will's sobs had subsided by the time he and Anke returned to the *daadi haus*, but he was shivering so she decided to give him a warm bath. It calmed him down, but afterward he hardly ate three bites of his supper.

"I'm tired. Can I go to bed?" he asked.

Since he was already in his pajamas, Anke said, "Yes. You can go into the living room and I'll come tuck you in in a moment." They had been carrying the battery-operated lamp from room to room, but now she lit a kerosene table lamp in the kitchen so Will could take Victor's lamp with him. She hastily finished her meal and then brought their dishes to the sink.

When she came into the living room, Will was already in bed. He was squeezing his eyes shut tightly, so she knew he wasn't really asleep. She sat down beside him and stroked his head. "Are you going to go to sleep without saying *gut nacht* to me?" she asked.

He opened his puffy eyelids. "Does that mean *good night* in Amish?"

"*Jah*—yes. The language we speak here is called *Deitsch*. Would you like me to teach you more *Deitsch* words?"

"*Jah*." He propped himself up on his elbow. "How do you say *mommy* in *Deitsch*?"

"*Mamm*," she replied softly.

"*Mamm*. That sounds kind of the same as *mom*." When he dropped back against his pillow again, Anke heard a faint but definite *clunk*.

"Uh-oh, I must have left something on your bed when I was making it up." She couldn't imagine what it could have been. A book? A kitchen utensil? She slid her hand under the pillow beneath his head.

"No, that's okay. You didn't leave any—" he started to protest.

Anke pulled out a framed, close-up photo of Clara and Will. It must have been what the *Englischers* called a "selfie," because it appeared to be taken at arm's length, above their heads. Clara had one arm wrapped around Will and they were both looking upward, grinning.

"Mommy—*Mamm* said I could keep it under my pillow. She said I could," he wailed, sucking his bottom lip in and out. Anke wanted to cry, too. She'd had her share of experience with young children and she knew even the best-behaved ones were prone to trying to get their way. Often, they used tears to do it. But this wasn't manipulation; this was a little boy expressing utter loneliness for his mother.

Their *Ordnung* prohibited the Amish to be photographed, but Anke thought, *Since he's not Amish, the* Ordnung *doesn't apply to him.* The *Ordnung* was less clear about whether that meant it was permissible for him to keep the photo in her house. Anke's sister was aware of that, too—it was probably why she'd instructed him to keep it hidden beneath his pillow. Or was it because she knew her son would feel loneliest at night?

Either way, Anke felt conflicted. She didn't want to encourage Will to hide the photo, because that seemed as if she'd be encouraging him to be deceptive. Nor did she feel it was prudent to allow him to display it openly, because it would offend her family and visitors. Finally, she handed him the photo and he hugged it to his chest. "You may keep it in your book bag for now and look at it before you go to sleep," she said. Careful not to use the word *hide* or *secret*, she added firmly, "When you're done looking at it, you can give it to me and

I'll put it in your backpack in the closet. You can see it again tomorrow night."

Will nodded. He pulled the frame away from his chest and studied it for a long moment before relinquishing it to Anke. She set it aside so she could tuck him in, taking another quilt from her bed and adding it to his. "You must miss your *mamm* very much, don't you?" she said, and he nodded again. "When your *mamm* moved away from me, I missed her very much, too. I still miss her a lot and it makes me sad. When that happens, do you know what I do?"

"Look at a picture of her?"

"*Neh.* Amish people don't have photos. But I do something even better than that. I pray to *Gott* and tell Him how sad I feel." Anke's voice wavered. She paused before continuing, "And sometimes He gives me a picture in my mind of your *mamm* smiling and that makes me not so lonely. I also ask *Gott* to keep her safe and not let her be too lonely, either. I think I'll do that now. Do you want to listen to me pray?"

"Should I close my eyes and do this?" He steepled his hands beneath his chin the way everyone had done while saying grace. Anke seized the opportunity to answer the question he'd interrupted Ernest's prayer with at supper.

"*Jah.* When we talk to *Gott*, we close our eyes and fold our hands because it helps us concentrate on Him. And we're very quiet because we want to hear each other praying."

"I'll be very quiet," Will said, so Anke prayed briefly for her sister and nephew and for herself, too.

When she finished she kissed him on the forehead and said good night and turned the lamp to the lowest setting. Then she went into the kitchen to clean the dishes. She spotted the container of cake on the counter, but she didn't feel in the mood for dessert. *It will just remind me of how hopeful I was and how joyful I felt that everything seemed to be going so well*, she thought.

Once she'd put the dishes away, she went into the living room to complete an apron she'd nearly finished making. *If I can sell a few more of these this week, I should have enough cash to buy Will a warmer coat*, she figured. But the light was too dim for sewing and she had to give up.

Although it was still early, she was so weary and cold she decided she might as well go to bed. As she lay in the dark listening to Will breathe, she ruminated over what had happened at the supper table. She appreciated that Velda was sensitive about the boy's behavior. It wouldn't be good if Asher, Micah and Millie began to imitate Will and interrupted the adults while they were praying. Or if they refused to obey an adult's instructions the first time they were told them, the way Amish children were taught to do from a very young age. But Anke felt resentful that Velda had been so stern about his conduct, considering it was Will's first evening in a new culture with complete strangers.

It wasn't as if Anke had any intention of allowing him to continue to have tantrums at the table, or anyplace else, for that matter. But if he didn't know what was acceptable and what wasn't, how could he be expected to follow the rules? That was why Anke had planned to take him into another room and speak to him in private. But when Velda butted in and chastised him so shrilly, she'd made matters worse. *I guess it's best for everyone if I don't bring Will to the* haus *anymore until I've spent some time helping him understand what's permissible and what isn't*, she decided. Not that her sister-in-law necessarily wanted her and Will to visit anyway, but Anke knew it was unrealistic to keep the children apart indefinitely.

At least Ernest seemed to be a little more patient with Will than Velda was. And if Anke wasn't mistaken, Josiah had seemed sympathetic, too, even though it must have been uncomfortable for him to be in the middle of such a tense family situation. *He really is a kind mann. Honor would be very fortunate to have him for a suitor*, she thought.

But as she pictured Honor riding in Josiah's buggy the way Anke had done that morning, she felt a peculiar heaviness in the pit of her stomach. It couldn't be envy, could it? *Neh*, she told herself. *It's just because I ate supper when I was upset.* So she clutched a pillow against her stomach, rolled over and went to sleep.

Josiah waited an extra hour before going to Anke's in the morning. He figured that she and Will might not have gotten a good night's rest and needed to sleep in. But when he arrived, he found them both in the barn, where he stabled his horse because the weather was too cold to tie him to the post outside.

"Good morning," he greeted them in *Englisch* after he'd unhitched the buggy.

"Gudermariye," they both said in unison.

Anke had dark circles beneath her eyes, but her cheeks were rosy and she was smiling. "Will's learning to speak *Deitsch*," she explained.

"And I learned to *millich* the *kieh*," he added happily, using the plural form of *cow* as the three of them walked outside into the bright sunlight. "*Onkel* Ernest showed me. *Ant* Anke and I collected *oier* from the *hinkel*, too."

After Will took off across the snowy yard toward the *daadi haus*, Josiah remarked, "You must have gotten up pretty early for him to *millich* the *kieh* with Ernest. I thought you might have needed some extra sleep. Otherwise I would have been here at my usual time."

"I'm just glad you came back after last night's supper," Anke said softly. From the lines on her forehead, Josiah could tell she was serious. He was touched that she was so concerned about his comfort, when she was the one dealing with so much. "I'm sorry if it was upsetting for you to be in the midst of all that…that chaos."

"Don't apologize. I have eight young nephews and nieces in Illinois, so I know that not every *familye* meal is a picnic."

"I'll have to remember that—not every *familye* meal is a picnic," Anke said with a chuckle. "I hope you at least enjoyed the *kuche*?"

Josiah had only eaten a small piece and honestly, he'd hardly recalled swallowing it. He didn't want to offend Anke, nor did he want to lie. "I, um…"

"Be honest—it was dry, wasn't it? I was afraid of that. It's such a rich cake that I worry about getting it done enough. As a result, sometimes I keep it in the oven too long."

He stopped walking and met her eyes. "*Neh*. It wasn't dry. Or if it was, I didn't notice. I sort of ate it fast and then I left, so…"

"Ah, I see. I hardly remember eating supper when I got back to the *daadi haus*, either. However, I saved my dessert. I know you don't like to take breaks when you're working, but you can have my slice with your lunch. If you like chocolate, I think you'll really enjoy it." She looked expectantly at him. Josiah noticed that instead of appearing greenish, today her eyes were closer to the frosty-blue color of the sky.

"Actually, I don't know if I can wait until lunchtime. I'm already *hungerich*," he said. "But I don't want to eat your entire dessert, because then you won't have any. Let's share it when I'm done repairing the sills on windows in the front bedroom, okay?"

"Perfect." Anke turned and they continued walking toward the *daadi haus* where Will was climbing the porch stairs.

"I should add another step. Those are too high. He can hardly get up that first one."

"*Jah*. Neither can Micah and Millie. They have to use their hands to boost themselves up. It reminds me of bear cubs climbing trees."

When Will had reached the top, he turned

around and called, "*Ant* Anke, how do you say *log cabin* in Amish?"

"*Daadi haus*," she called back. When Josiah tipped his head at her, confused, she waved her hand and said, "Don't ask, cowboy." Her answer gave Josiah such a belly laugh he had to stop to clutch his sides.

"What's funny?" Will questioned.

"We're both just very *hallich* this morning," his aunt answered.

"I'm *hallich*, too," Will said and from the smile on his face, Josiah knew he understood what *hallich* meant.

For the next couple of hours as Josiah worked in the front bedroom, he could hear Will asking Anke questions. She never seemed to get exasperated, even though her nephew was far more outspoken about his curiosity than most Amish children Josiah knew in his district. But then, Will probably had more questions because he hadn't grown up in this culture. *I might be a newcomer to this district, but Will's a newcomer to this entire lifestyle*, Josiah realized. *For such a young bu, he's awfully brave.*

After a while, Anke's and Will's voices died down and then he heard the front door close and he figured they went outside. They were back within fifteen minutes, no doubt because the boy's flimsy jacket didn't keep him warm enough in the subfreezing temperatures. Josiah waited a few minutes so they could warm up by the stove before he emerged from the bedroom and announced, "I'm *hallich* you're back. I was about to take a break."

Anke put on a pot of coffee and warmed some milk for Will. She was going to split her slice of cake between Josiah and her, and allow her nephew to eat the smaller slice she'd cut for him. But Will insisted he wanted to share his cake with Josiah, too. Since the child was still cold, Anke suggested they eat in front of the woodstove. Will allowed Josiah to use the armchair and he dragged in a chair from the kitchen. Anke sat in the rocker.

"Do you think Asher and Micah and Millie are going to *kumme* outside and play with me pretty soon?" Will asked his aunt with his mouth full.

"It's not polite to speak when you have food in your mouth, Will," she said, holding a finger to her lips. "I don't know if your *ant* Velda will allow your *gschwischderkinner* to play outside today. It might be too cold."

"Aww." Will opened his mouth again to complain, even though he hadn't swallowed his cake.

"You know what I like to do when I'm eating *kuche* that tastes as *appenditlich* as this tastes, Will?" Josiah asked, so Anke wouldn't have to correct the child again. "I like to take a nice big bite—not too big, but big enough to taste the frosting *and* the cake—and I just let it melt in my mouth for as long as I can. That way, all of my taste buds can really enjoy how sweet and rich it is. Like this." He showed Will what he meant and the boy imitated him.

After that, the three of them quietly ate their cake, with no sound except for the fire crackling and their forks scraping against their plates. After he'd taken the last bite, savoring its dense, chocolate texture, Josiah glanced up to see Anke watching him. He smiled and gave her a satisfied nod to indicate how much he enjoyed the dessert.

Actually, it wasn't just the dessert he enjoyed; it was the coziness of the fire and the pleasure of being in Anke's and Will's company. Unfortunately, ever since the incident at the golf course, Josiah was on the defensive, so he rarely felt this relaxed around anyone outside his family. While Anke and Will continued to eat their cake, he stretched his legs out in front of him, in no hurry to get back to work.

"That was *gut*," Will said, smearing chocolate across his face as he wiped his lips with the back of his hand. Anke handed him a napkin.

"That's for sure," Josiah agreed.

"*Denki*. I'm *hallich* you both enjoyed it."

She had no sooner finished her sentence than there was a knock on the door. Will flew across the room to open it before Anke could put her plate down. It was Honor Bawell, of all people, and she was holding a plastic container in her hands.

"*Gudermariye*," Will exuberantly greeted their visitor.

Anke shot across the room behind him and Josiah hopped up from his chair, too. "*Gudermariye*, Honor," she echoed.

"Hello, Anke. Hi, Josiah." Honor looked down at the boy. In *Englisch* she asked, "Are you Clara's son?"

"*Jah*. This is Will, my nephew," Anke piped up.

"I can get a chair for you," the child offered Honor.

"*Neh*. She can use mine. I need to get back to work," Josiah said.

"You do? But I made Long John Rolls." She held up the container. "They're best when they're eaten fresh."

Ordinarily, it was true; the oblong frosted donuts were best when eaten the same day they were made. However, Anke knew there was

no good day to eat anything Honor baked—
she had an uncanny talent for ruining virtu-
ally every recipe she attempted. As her own
mother once joked, "Honor can't serve a cup of
kaffi without getting eggshells in it." But that
didn't stop her from trying and from handing
out her confections to unsuspecting bachelors
like Josiah. Anke hoped for his sake he was
too full to accept.

"What's a Long John Roll?" Will asked.

"It's a doughnut with frosting on the top, but
it's long instead of round," Anke explained in
Englisch.

"Yum. Can I try one, please?"

"You've just had a piece of *kuche*. No more
sweets for you," his aunt told him.

"I've just had a piece of *kuche*, too, so I'll
have to pass," Josiah said, putting on his coat.
"I'm going to be working on the window frame
from outdoors."

Honor's face fell. "That's too bad, but I'll
leave you these for later. By the way, did you
find out if your *bruder* has snowshoes?"

"Uh, I believe I saw a pair hanging in the
mudroom, *jah*."

"*Wunderbaar!* We've got another trek planned
this *Sundaag*. We're meeting at the gorge at one
thirty, after everyone has finished their home
worship services and eaten lunch."

"Oh, well, I..."

"You can't say *neh*. You promised me, remember?"

Josiah promised Honor he'd go snowshoeing with her? Anke wondered. *Is that why he's turning red—because he's interested in her already?*

"*Jah*, that's right. I'll be there, weather permitting." Josiah walked toward the door, but Honor was in his way, and as he tried to go around her, she stepped in the same direction. When she moved to the other side at the same time he did, accidentally blocking him again, she giggled. "Excuse me," he mumbled and squeezed by her and out the door.

Honor unbuttoned her coat and began to take it off, but then changed her mind. "It's chilly in here. I'll keep this on while we're having *kaffi*," she said, which meant she was staying.

She's never kumme *to visit me at this time on a weekday before*, Anke thought as she went into the kitchen to pour Honor a cup of coffee. *I'm sure her primary purpose in coming was to see Josiah, not me. Not that I care—I told her I didn't mind if they ended up courting and I meant it.* But she, Josiah and Will were having such a nice, peaceful time together that Anke wished it hadn't been cut short.

When she returned to the living room, she

found Will reciting all the Amish words he knew to Honor. How was Anke going to keep him occupied while the two women were visiting? Like most Amish people, she didn't believe a child should be privy to adult conversation, nor did she believe children should have to be constantly entertained. However, she couldn't send him to one of the bedrooms, because both of them were in various states of disrepair and they were drafty. Nor could she send him outside to play because it was too cold. Once again, she wished she would have checked some picture books out of the library.

After serving Honor coffee, Anke asked Will to come into the kitchen. "While I'm visiting with my friend, you may sit in here and use these crayons to draw a picture for Asher and Millie and Micah, since they made Valentine's Day cards for us." This morning, she and Will had opened them and taped them to the wall above the boy's bed. Since the children were so young, it was difficult to tell what they had drawn, but the pictures added a splash of color to the room.

Once Anke had Will situated, she returned to the living room to visit with Honor, who chattered almost nonstop. After an hour she wished her visitor would be on her way. But because Anke was no longer responsible for keeping a big house and she wasn't helping Velda care for her children, she didn't have any pressing reason to excuse herself. *I hope Honor doesn't stay until lunchtime in hope of visiting with Josiah during his break*, she thought.

Fortunately, Will came into the living room a few minutes later. "I finished all my pictures. Want to see them?"

Impressed that he'd been working so intently for this long by himself, Anke said, "*Jah.* Show us what you drew."

Although childlike, his pictures had an astonishing amount of detail for someone so young. Even if he hadn't announced what he'd drawn as he presented each sheet of paper, Anke would have been able to discern what he'd depicted. A mother rabbit with a baby bunny for Charity. Two birds in a tree for Millie—the tree also had a wooden swing, like the one Anke had shown him Clara used to swing on. A frog and a dog for Micah.

"This is for Asher," he said, holding up the last one.

Anke immediately recognized what he'd meant to illustrate, but Honor questioned, "What are all those horses pulling? A plough?"

"Those aren't *geil*," he told her, recalling the Amish word for horses that Anke had taught him. "They're reindeer. That's Santa's sleigh. See? He's got lots of presents."

Honor's eyes grew wide. To Anke, she said, "You're not going to let him give Asher that, are you?"

Anke discreetly shook her head, but Will caught her. Wide-eyed, he cocked his head and said, "But I made it for him."

"I'll explain after Honor leaves," Anke said pointedly, standing up and retrieving her and Will's coats from the closet. "Let's walk her to her buggy, Will. We can see her *gaul*."

The promise of seeing a horse was enough to temporarily distract Will. He set the pictures on his bed and hurried to put his coat on. When they stepped outside, Honor said, "I'm just going to pop around the corner to say goodbye to Josiah. You go ahead and show your nephew my *gaul*. I'll be right there."

It's one thing if she wants to speak with Josiah in private, but she should do that on her own time, Anke thought, annoyed that Honor was dismissing her as if *she* was the visitor. *It reminds me of how I felt about being in my own* haus *yesterday evening.* But since she wanted to be a good example to her nephew, Anke complied and led him to the barn so Honor could be alone with Josiah.

* * *

I should have brought the stepladder out here, Josiah thought, stretching to pound a stubborn nail into the window frame. He didn't hear anyone approach so he flinched when Honor touched his shoulder. "Sorry," she said. "I said your name, but you didn't answer."

"You're fortunate I didn't swing my hammer farther back than I did or you might have gotten a black eye," he told her, and she laughed, as if he was trying to be funny. Honor didn't seem to have any more sense about safety than Velda did.

"I'm leaving now, but I wanted you to know that Anke put your Long John Rolls in the kitchen—I hope she doesn't allow her nephew to get into them. He doesn't seem to understand what's forbidden here."

Of course he doesn't. He hasn't even been here for twenty-four hours, Josiah thought. "*Denki.* I'll take them home with me. Bye, Honor."

She didn't budge. "I also wanted to remind you about snowshoeing at the gorge. One thirty on *Sundaag*. Okay?"

"*Jah.* I said I'd be there and I will."

"Because you always keep your word," she said, giggling as if it was some kind of private joke between them.

Josiah turned back to the window frame and raised the hammer. "Watch yourself. You're too close," he warned. So she stepped away, said goodbye and finally left.

Josiah was frustrated for a number of reasons. First, as careful as he was being in his work on the *daadi haus*, he regretted repatching the holes in the roof and essentially tacking on windows. The place needed a complete overhaul, not just a few cover-ups here and there. Second, he was really cold and he wouldn't have come outside at all to work right now if Honor hadn't stopped by. Third, he wished he hadn't committed to going snowshoeing with her and the other singles their age. He didn't intend to be vain, but it was relatively clear to him that Honor was behaving flirtatiously toward him.

And Josiah was *not* interested in courting again. But if he was, it wouldn't be with someone like her. Honor was certainly attractive and generous and friendly. But he preferred someone who didn't seem so…so frivolous. Someone who had priorities that she pursued as intently as she pursued a suitor. Someone who was more mature. Someone like Anke.

Where did that thought kumme *from?* he asked himself. *This cold weather must be getting to me.* His fingers were numb and he couldn't get anything else done out here, so he headed inside. As usual, he closed the bedroom door behind him to prevent the warm air from escaping from the living room. A few minutes later, he heard Anke and Will come in.

"Can we bring my pictures to my *gschwischderkind* before we take our coats off?

"*Neh*. It's almost time for lunch," Anke said, but Josiah guessed she was stalling. He could have been wrong, but from the little he knew of Velda, he figured it would be a while before she'd let Will play with her children again.

"After lunch?"

"*Kumme* sit here with me, Will," Anke said. Even though Josiah knew he shouldn't listen in, the softness of her voice made him curious. "I like the pictures you made for Micah, Millie and Charity. But Amish *kinner* don't believe in Santa Claus, so I'm afraid you can't give the picture of the reindeer to Asher."

"But...but if he doesn't believe in Santa Claus, who gives him presents at Christmas?"

"Well, his *mamm* and *daed* give him a gift. I do, too. But Amish people celebrate *Grischtdaag*—that means Christmas—by worshipping *Gott*. We sing and pray and at *schul* the *kinner* have a pageant, which is a lot of fun. And we have *gut* things to eat and we spend time with our friends and *familye*."

In the long pause that followed, he imagined Will was trying to absorb what Anke had told him. Josiah didn't move, afraid that it would be obvious he'd been eavesdropping. Finally, Will said, "If I draw a picture of something else for Asher, then can we take them to my *gschwischderkind* after lunch?"

"We'll see."

"But I won't draw Santa—"

"Will." Anke's voice was firm. "When an adult gives you an answer, you may not argue with them. Do you understand me?"

He must have nodded because the next thing Josiah heard Anke say was that he should go wash his hands so he could help her crack eggs into the pan for lunch.

"Oier?" he asked.

"Jah. That's right. *Oier.* Very *gut."*

When he heard footsteps scampering down the hall, Josiah resumed his assessment of the work he still needed to complete on the window. But first, he was going to have his lunch. He set down his hammer on the sill and the entire board fell off from the tool's weight. "Arg," he moaned, louder than he'd intended.

The door suddenly opened and Anke questioned, "Are you okay?"

"Jah. But this sill isn't." He pointed to it.

She chuckled. "That must be exasperating,

but I'm *hallich* it's only the wood that fell off and nothing happened to you."

"*Jah.* At least the window is reparable, so I shouldn't be upset. But I think I need to take my lunch break now. I'll be back when I'm done."

"Did you leave your lunch in your buggy? It will be frozen. You're *wilkom* to join Will and me for scrambled *oier.*"

Josiah hesitated. Usually he ate his lunch in the barn, because he hadn't wanted to give her the impression he was interested in socializing with her. Nor did he want Velda to read anything into his actions and decide he was siding with Anke. But now that he'd been a guest at the Bachmans' table, Josiah wasn't as worried anymore about what Velda thought of him. And this morning it had been so pleasant taking a break indoors with Anke and her nephew. *Why not?* he asked himself.

To Anke, he said, "*Denki.* That sounds *gut.*"

In fact, it sounded terrific.

Chapter Six

After four days, Anke still hadn't seen Velda or the children outside once, not even to hang her laundry. *She must be hanging her clothes in the basement to dry because it's so cold outside,* she thought. But Anke couldn't entirely rid her mind of the nagging feeling that her sister-in-law didn't *want* to see her. Or, more likely, that she didn't want her children to see Will. Anke wouldn't push, since she had previously agreed she wouldn't visit the house with Will without an invitation. However, by Thursday, she needed to retrieve additional sewing supplies and material from her room.

She decided she'd run over to the house while Josiah and Will were eating, since he agreed to keep an eye on the boy while she was gone. Josiah had been joining them inside for lunch all week. Sometimes he brought his own

Velda finally turned around to face her and Anke noticed immediately how frazzled she appeared. Also, she had something—oatmeal?—crusted on her forehead. "Okay, I'll give him another chance. But you'll have to supervise them, because as you can see, after lunch, I still have breakfast dishes to do."

Anke was so thrilled that Velda was allowing the children to play together that she offered, "If we let the *kinner* play indoors, I could do the dishes and you could take a nap. You look a little tired. Besides, it's so cold out there."

"I shouldn't nap. I have laundry I haven't put through the wringer, yet."

Anke recognized a hint when she heard one, but again, all she could think about was how happy Will and his cousins were going to be to spend time together. "I'll take care of that, too. It's fine."

"Oh, all right," Velda said with a sigh, as if she was the one doing Anke a favor instead of the other way around.

Asher trudged back into the room with Anke's canvas bag and Micah and Millie followed on his heels. They enveloped their aunt from opposite sides of her legs and told her they'd missed her, too, just as Asher had done.

"Guess what? When you're done eating your

supp, I'm going to bring Will back here to play with you."

The three children's cheers startled Charity and she flung a handful of banana onto the floor.

"Now look what you made her do!" Velda scolded and Anke wasn't sure whether the comment was directed at her or the children.

She really must be exhausted to be so easily agitated, Anke thought. *The sooner she takes a nap, the better for everyone.* "It's okay. I'll wipe it up." When she was done, she hurried back to the *daadi haus* to tell Will the good news.

"Where's your bag?" he asked and Anke noticed his mouth was full. Fortunately, he wouldn't be eating at the main house, so she still had time to work with him on table manners.

"I was so excited I forgot it at your *ant* Velda's."

"Why are you excited?"

"Because she invited you over to play with your *gschwischderkinner*!"

Instead of the joyful outburst she was expecting, Will knitted his brows together. "Aren't you coming with me?"

Anke noticed that his question made Josiah wince. Like Anke, he must have recognized that Will was apprehensive about receiving another scolding from Velda. "*Jah.* Of course, I'm coming with you. I'm going to help do *Ant* Velda's housework while she's napping. Maybe I'll have time to work on my aprons, too."

"I'll bring my pictures." Will had made a second drawing for Asher to replace the first; this one was of two boys chasing chickens.

"First, go wash your hands so you don't get them sticky."

After Will left the room, Anke said, "*Denki* for keeping him company while I was gone, Josiah."

"It was no trouble."

"Did he ask you one hundred and one questions?"

"One hundred and two," Josiah joked, his blue eyes twinkling. "But it was fine. He's just trying to make sense of his new world."

If Honor had asked me today what Josiah is like, I would say he's very patient and understanding and he's got a gut *sense of humor*, Anke mused, recalling the question her friend had posed to her in the kitchen at church. To Josiah, she said, "Still, he's so curious that it can be tiresome for an *eldre* to respond to him after a while. At least, I feel that way sometimes. I'm *hallich* I'll get a little break while he's playing with his *gschwischderkinner.*"

"Seems to me that Velda's the one getting the break, not you."

Anke didn't understand what he meant at first and then she realized she'd mentioned she was going to help Velda with her housework. "Oh, I don't mind doing a few dishes. I'm so used to managing a bigger household that it feels strange for me just to have two people to clean up after. My *schweschder*-in-law looked utterly beat and I know she'll feel better after a nap. Besides, I'd gladly clean the *haus* from top to bottom if that's what it takes for Will and his *gschwischderkinner* to spend time together."

I know you would. Your dedication to doing what's best for Will—and for others—is one of your most winsome qualities, Josiah thought, peering into Anke's eyes. He couldn't say it, though, so he broke his gaze and stood up. "I'm going into town to pick up some PVC windowsill protectors. They'll last longer than these wooden sills. Is there anything else you need at the hardware store while I'm there?"

"*Neh*. But *denki* for asking."

Will returned to the room and the three of them put on their coats and stepped outside at the same time. Josiah noticed the boy was pulling on Anke's hand like a puppy on a leash, dragging her toward the main house.

Dear Lord, he's so excited—please help him to have a gut *time and for everyone, including Velda, to be kind and forbearing to each other,* he prayed as he walked toward the barn to hitch his horse and buggy and ride into town.

Josiah entered the hardware store less than half an hour later, just as Ben Nisley, Victor's nearest neighbor in New Hope, was coming toward the exit. The men stopped to greet each other and exchange small talk before Ben said, "My wife and I are aware you're on your own for a while. Would you like to join us for worship this *Sundaag*?"

The Amish only met together for worship every other week. On "off-Sundays" they met with their immediate family members in their own homes. Because Josiah was alone and didn't have anyone to worship with, he gratefully accepted Ben's offer. "I'd appreciate that. But I made a commitment to go snowshoeing at one thirty—will your wife be offended if I leave right after lunch?"

"*Neh.* Of course not. She's still young enough to remember what it was like when we were courting age—she'll be *hallich* you're getting out and having *schpass* with your peers."

Although Josiah was surprised by Ben's mention of courting, he let the comment pass. After saying goodbye, he browsed the aisles until he found the windowsill protectors he'd come to buy and set them on the register in front of Keith.

"I heard you making plans to worship with Ben's *familye* on *Sundaag*," Keith remarked. "Is Anke going, too?"

"Anke? Why would she worship with the Nisleys? She lives clear across town from them."

"*Jah*, but birds of a feather."

"What do you mean by that?"

He shrugged. "You know. The Nisleys rent out their *daadi haus* to *Englischers* and Anke allows her *Englisch* alcoholic *schweschder*'s *suh* to stay in hers. My *schweschder*-in-law Ruth said Anke won't be allowed to worship with her *familye* on *Sundaag* since Velda doesn't want her nephew being part of their service. I figured the only people who might not mind if she brings the *bu* with her would be the Nisleys—and you."

Josiah responded quietly but firmly. "As far as I know, Anke won't be worshipping with us. But neither the Nisley *familye* nor Anke is violating the *Ordnung* because it's not a violation to allow a guest to worship with the members of this district on occasion, whether at home or in *kurrich.*"

Omer Wilford, the man whose workshop Josiah had helped raise the previous Saturday, had come up to the counter beside Will. "It may not be a violation of the *Ordnung*, but that doesn't mean it's a *gut* idea," he interjected. "Frankly, I'm surprised Iddo Stoll didn't discourage Anke more strongly from taking the *bu* in. It seems unfair to those *familye* with small *kinner* that just because she has chosen to allow an *Englischer* into her *haus*, the rest of the district has to allow him into our worship services."

"He's only a young *bu* and he won't be in New Hope for very long. I don't think he'll lead the other *kinner* astray," Josiah argued. "Most of them don't even speak *Englisch* well enough to converse with him."

"They don't have to speak with him—temptation usually starts with the eyes," Omer said. "My *kinner* are old enough to recognize the differences between the *Englisch* and the Amish. It might seem innocent on the surface to invite an *Englischer* to worship with us, but before we know it, our *kinner* will want to wear bright clothes and talk on cell phones, too."

Will is only five years old so he doesn't have

a cell phone—but both of you *do. Even if you only use them for business purposes, your* kinner *might be just as tempted to wish they had a cell phone by watching you make calls as they are by anything Will does*, Josiah thought. But he felt too intimidated to voice his opinion.

"It's not just young *kinner* who can be led astray by socializing or worshipping with *Englischers*." Keith stared directly at Josiah, even though he was replying to Omer. "If *eldre* spend too much time around *Englischers*, they can be tempted to blur the lines between the world and us, too. Especially when it involves someone an Amish person cares about, the way Anke cares about her alcoholic *schweschder*. But it's not long before a person starts making excuses and compromises they wouldn't have made if they'd stayed away from the *Englisch* altogether."

"Amen!" Omer uttered. "That's why I'm opposed to an *Englischer* living in our community. I sure won't let my *kinner* go anywhere around the *bu*—or even around other *kinner* who go around the *bu*. And I intend to arrive early to *kurrich* and sit in the front row so my *kinner* won't be able to see Anke's nephew."

Keith snickered. "Problem is, there are so many other people in the district who feel the same way that the front bench might already be filled, no matter how early you get to *kurrich*."

When Omer cracked up, Josiah forced himself to chuckle, too. Then he paid for his purchase and said goodbye. He hurried out the door and down the street to his buggy, his stomach churning. It was clear to him that no matter how fond he was growing of Will and Anke, he had to distance himself from them. If he didn't, other people in his new community would distance themselves from *him* and he'd wind up as miserable in New Hope as he'd been in Illinois.

I can't fault Velda for napping for so long, Anke thought. *I'm the one who told her to sleep as long as she needed to.* But she would have weighed her words more carefully if she'd known her sister-in-law was going to sleep for almost three hours.

During that time, Anke had washed, dried and put away the breakfast and lunch dishes, as well as run the laundry through the wringer and hung it up in the basement to dry. She'd also scrubbed the kitchen floor, which was encrusted with the same oatmeal she'd noticed on Velda's forehead, and cleaned the bathroom.

She'd completed most of these tasks while

lugging Charity around on her hip—the baby was unusually clingy because she needed a nap, but she refused to take one. Anke didn't want her wailing to disturb Velda's rest, so she gave up trying to put her down. In between these chores, Anke had supervised the children as they'd colored and played with blocks. She'd also let them help her scrub potatoes for supper, which really amounted to allowing them to splash around in the sink. Finally, Charity fell asleep, so after putting her in the crib upstairs, Anke suggested the children quietly look at the books Velda had checked out of the library.

Anke had barely sat down and sewn ten stitches on an apron hem when she heard Charity fussing. She went upstairs again to discover the baby was in urgent need of a diaper change. As Anke cleaned her up, she could hear the children getting rambunctious downstairs, but by that time, she didn't care if they woke Velda, so she continued dressing the infant. Now Charity was wide awake, so Anke decided to take her back downstairs.

"Did you have a *gut* rest?" she asked when she saw Velda coming out of her bedroom.

"*Jah*—until the *kinner* woke me up. What in the world are they doing down there?"

"They were reading when I came to see why

the *bobbel* was fussing." Anke followed Velda down the stairs.

When they entered the gathering room, they found Micah and Millie sitting on the floor, clapping in awe as Asher and Will jumped so high on the couch it seemed their heads would hit the ceiling. For some reason, Will had the apron Anke had been sewing tied around his neck.

"Absatz!" Velda commanded sharply and Asher immediately stopped jumping and landed on his bottom on the couch cushion. Velda repeated the Amish word, louder this time. *"Absatz!"*

"That means *stop*, Will," Anke told him. He immediately stopped jumping, too. Anke thrust Charity into Velda's arms and walked over to where the boys were sitting on the couch, both red-faced and staring at their knees. Untying her apron from Will's neck, she said, "Hold still or you'll stick yourself—this has pins in it. What were you thinking to tie it around your neck?"

"It's my cape. I was being a superhero so I could jump higher than Asher."

Velda gasped. "That's it. I want that *bu* out of this house right now. It's bad enough that he got Asher to jump on the couch, but introducing him to such nonsense as a superhero is inexcusable. He is *not* allowed to be around my *kinner* again," she ranted to Anke in *Deitsch*.

Although Will couldn't have understood what she'd said, Asher burst into tears and then Micah and Millie did, too. "But, *Mamm*—" Asher began to object.

Velda snapped her fingers and pointed at her son. "Quiet," she said, silencing him before speaking to Anke in *Deitsch* again. "See? Look how much influence he's already had. My *kinner* are talking back to me and having tantrums because they saw *him* do it. I warned you and Ernest this would happen. But would you listen? *Neh!*"

"*Kumme*, Will. Let's go," Anke said, collecting her sewing bag on the way out of the room. They put on their hats, coats and mittens and walked back across the snowy lawn in silence, except for Will's sniffling. Anke glanced over and saw a few tears rolling down his cheeks, but she didn't console him. If he was crying because he regretted that he'd jumped on the couch and taken Anke's apron, then she considered his tears a sign of a healthy conscience.

Besides, she was too angry about the way Velda handled the situation to say anything comforting to Will. She thought both boys should have been admonished for jumping on the couch. Then Anke could have addressed the issue of Will taking her apron and super-heroes, too. *They deserved to be scolded, but banishing Will from the* haus *for the rest of the time he's here seems unnecessarily stringent,* she thought. *And Velda can't blame her* kin-ners' *crying on him—they're probably crying because they're tired. Or because* she's *been short-tempered with them lately.*

When they got inside, Anke realized Josiah had returned and was working in the next room. She hoped he didn't overhear their entire conversation. She'd been working so hard all week to help shape Will's behavior, but obviously, she hadn't done a good enough job of it and it made her feel like a failure.

After they'd taken off their coats, she told him to sit down. Standing in front of him, Anke asked, "Does your *mamm* allow you to jump on the couch in your apartment, Will?" She knew she couldn't really fault him for jumping on Velda's couch if he'd never been forbidden to do it at home.

He looked at her and shrugged his shoulders, fat tears beaded on his lashes.

"I want you to think about it and then answer *jah* or *neh*." She repeated, "Does your *mamm* allow you to jump on the couch at home?"

"I—I don't know. Our couch doesn't bounce.

It's called a futon. Mommy sleeps on it at night. It's kind of hard and it's got wood under it."

"I see." Anke noticed he'd reverted to calling his mother *mommy*. "Well, jumping on the furniture is not allowed here. In fact, you should never do it anywhere. Furniture is for sitting on. If you jump on it, you could get hurt. Or you could get the furniture dirty or even break it. You are not allowed to do that again. If you do, I'll take away your soft armchair and you can sit on a hard kitchen chair from now on so you won't be tempted to jump on it. Do you understand?"

"Jah." He hung his head and his tears splotched the legs of his pants.

Anke dropped into the rocking chair beside him. "Will, look at me." When he did, she said, "You're also not permitted to take anything that belongs to someone else without their permission. That's not right. How would you feel if someone went into your backpack and took something that belonged to you?"

Will cried harder, his chin quivering. "Please don't take my picture of Mommy, *Ant* Anke. Please? You said I could look at it at night. You said so."

Anke got up so she could lift the child onto her lap. Cradling him against her, she said, "I'm not going to take your photo, Will. I promise. I only asked you how you'd feel if I did take it. And I can tell it would make you very sad. That's how I felt when you took my apron."

As she rocked back and forth, a few tears rolled down her cheeks and dripped off her chin onto his fine blond locks. Anke was torn up inside because she knew how hard Will was trying to fit in and how much he missed his mother. She was also angry at her sister because the consequences of Clara's decisions were hurting her son even more than they'd hurt her Amish family. *Dear* Gott, *please heal Will's heart*, Anke prayed. *Help me to be a comfort to him and give me wisdom about how to guide him during his time here.*

Eventually, the boy quieted down and pulled back so he could look her in the eyes. "I'm sorry I took your apron, *Ant* Anke," he apologized.

"I forgive you. And I trust you not to take anything of mine again."

"I won't," he said, solemnly shaking his head.

Anke gave him a hug before she told him, "I know you might see superheroes on TV at home, but Amish *kinner* don't believe in superheroes who can fly or who have special powers to fight evil."

"They don't?"

"*Neh.* The only One who can do such mighty things is Jesus, or *Gott.* He can do miracles and He always opposes sin—that means the things people do and say and think that are wrong. Yet even though He hates sin, if we believe in Him, He forgives us for all those bad things. But Jesus is real and superheroes are pretend. That's one of the reasons *Ant* Velda got so upset—she doesn't want you telling Asher about someone who's make-believe."

"I didn't tell him. The book did."

Anke tipped her head. "What book?"

"From the library. It has a superhero cat in a cape in it. It's for the letter *C.*"

"So that's why you tied my apron around your neck?"

"*Jah.* I'm sorry." Will dropped his head again.

"It's okay. I said I forgave you and I did." She cupped Will's chin and lifted his head. "But I need to understand what happened. You tied my apron around your neck and then you jumped on *Ant* Velda's couch and Asher did, too?"

Will couldn't move his head because Anke was holding his chin, but he averted his eyes to the side and down, his lashes fanning his cheeks.

"Will, when I ask you a question, you must

answer me. Who jumped on the couch first? You or Asher?"

"Asher." His voice was raspy as he added, "He said he could jump higher than a super-hero because he ate a whole lot of steak at supper."

Anke tensed her jaw, absorbing what she'd discovered. It occurred to her that Asher had tried to tell his mother what had really happened, but she had silenced him. *This* was the very reason why Anke had wanted to speak to the boys about what they'd done, instead of flying off the handle like Velda. "Okay, well, we'll talk to your *ant* about this later."

"So I can say sorry about jumping on the couch?"

"*Jah*, that's one reason." Anke touched the tip of his turned-up nose. *I just hope Velda is as contrite about her mistake as you are*, she thought.

From what he'd overheard of Anke and Will's conversation, Josiah could picture the events that unfolded at Velda's house earlier in the afternoon. He sympathized with her and the boy because it sounded as if Will had been blamed for something that wasn't entirely his fault. He'd been listening to Anke instruct her nephew all week in the ways of the Amish and he had no doubt that she was committed to helping him fit in. More important, she was clearly teaching him about God's love and forgiveness.

But he couldn't deny it troubled him to hear her and Will talk about a photo in his book bag. From what Josiah deduced, it seemed she was allowing him to take the photo out when no one else was around and that seemed deceptive. He recalled what Keith had said about how Amish adults were sometimes tempted to make excuses for *Englischers*, especially *Englischers* they spent a lot of time with or cared deeply about.

I think that may be what's happening with Anke and her schweschder *and nephew*, he thought. *In a way, it happened to me, too—I got involved with* Englischers *when I tried to help Jana's* bruder. *I would have been better off if I had just kept going past the golf course that day.*

Anke and Will's conversation reaffirmed what Josiah had decided earlier that afternoon; he was going to have to severely limit his connection to them. That meant no more lunch breaks together anymore. While Josiah didn't relish the idea of eating in the barn again, on the plus side, the cold weather would force him to take a quicker break, which meant he'd finish his work on the *daadi haus* quicker, too. He estimated that he could complete everything by Friday or Saturday of next week, if he hurried.

After that, the only time I'll see Anke and her nephew will be in kurrich—*unless I sit in the front row so I won't be led astray by the sight of them, too*, he thought wryly.

Chapter Seven

"Why isn't Josiah eating lunch with us today?" Will asked on Friday afternoon when he returned from washing his hands and discovered that Josiah had left for the barn.

I don't know, Anke thought. *But he certainly has been acting odd. Yesterday he hardly uttered goodbye when he left and this morning he barely greeted us, either. He must have something on his mind.* She'd considered asking him if anything was wrong, but she didn't want to pry, especially not with Will around.

"He said he wanted to check to be sure his *gaul*'s water isn't frozen. He wasn't planning to take a very long break anyway."

"Can we go to *Ant* Velda and *Onkel* Ernest's *haus* after lunch?"

Anke was impressed by Will's self-restraint. Even though she knew he was eager to see his cousins again, this was the first time he'd asked her about it today. But Anke had decided to wait until tomorrow to go over to the main house, since Ernest only worked until noon on Saturdays. She figured it would be better to discuss the boys' behavior when her brother was present, as he was more reasonable and calmer than Velda was.

Also, Saturday afternoon was when either Velda or Anke would typically use the buggy to go to the supermarket, while the other woman stayed home and watched the children. So Anke would have to go to the house anyway, to either give her grocery list to Velda, or to get Velda's list from her.

"We're going to their *haus* tomorrow, when *Onkel* Ernest gets home from his butcher shop."

"But why can't—" Will started to ask and then he clamped his hand over his mouth, apparently remembering he wasn't supposed to argue with a grown-up's decision. From behind his fingers he mumbled, "I forgot."

"That's okay. We all forget what we're supposed to do or what we're not supposed to do sometimes. But if we practice, it becomes a habit and after a while, we don't even have to think about it—we just do what we're supposed to do," Anke said. "Now, let's bow our heads and I'll say grace."

"Don't forget to pray for *Mamm*," Will reminded her, just as he'd done at every meal and again every evening when she prayed with him before he went to bed.

"Dear *Gott*," she prayed. She could hear the front door open and close again—Josiah must have returned from the barn. She waited for his footsteps to fade as he walked into the bedroom before continuing, "*Denki* for this food and for Your love. Please help us to do the things we should and to repent when we do the things we shouldn't. Please heal Clara in all the ways she needs healing and bring her home to us soon. Amen."

"How many more days until I get to see Mommy?" Will asked when he opened his eyes. Anke noticed he always reverted to the *Englisch* word when he felt lonely.

Clara hadn't even been in the recovery program for a week yet, so Anke didn't want to discourage Will by saying he had thirty-some days left before she came home. Instead she told him, "In about five weeks."

"Is that a really lot of days? Is it this many?" He held up all ten of his fingers.

"*Neh*. It's more than that."

His jaw dropped. "But that's too many days."

"I know it seems that way, *jah*. But sometimes it takes that long for…for someone to get completely better. Otherwise, if they leave the hospital too soon, they might end up getting sick again and then they'd have to go back into the hospital. We don't want that to happen." Anke gestured toward Will's bowl, hoping to distract him. "Your *supp* is getting cold."

He picked up his spoon and stirred the broth, but he didn't lift it to his mouth. "If *Mamm* eats lots of steak, will she get better?"

Now Anke felt too sad to eat, too. She set down her spoon. "Your *mamm* needs more than protein to get better. She needs help from the people at the hospital."

"Can't *Gott* help her get better?"

"Absolutely. That's why we pray about it every day and every night. But even with *Gott*'s help, sometimes it takes a while for a person to get better." Anke knew the conversation was becoming too intense for the child, so she said, "I know you want to see your *mamm* very soon and so do I. But I'm glad that while we're waiting for her to *kumme* back, we get to be together. I love having you here and teaching you about being Amish. And I also have lots to do, so I really need your help."

"You do?" Will slurped a spoonful of his soup. "Like what?"

"I want to make snickerdoodle *kuchen* this afternoon and I'd like you to crack the *oier* for me."

"Okay. I'm *gut* at mixing, too." Will's countenance brightened considerably.

"Ah, but are you as *gut* at eating *kuchen* as you are at making them?"

He giggled. "*Jah.* I can eat this many." He held up his ten fingers again.

"That many? You'd get a *bauchweh* if you ate ten *kuchen*."

"Does that mean a tummy ache?"

"*Jah.*"

"Then I won't eat ten. I can give some to Josiah."

"What a *wunderbaar* idea," Anke exclaimed.

But at the end of the day when Will presented the cookies to him, Josiah's half-hearted thanks made Anke wish they had saved the cookies for themselves. *Can't he see how eager Will is to share with him?* she thought. *I don't care if Josiah got up on the wrong side of the bed or not. He could show a little more enthusiasm than that when a* kind *gives him something he made.*

"I don't think he likes snickerdoodles," the boy surmised after Josiah left. "Maybe he's 'lergic."

"That could be. But maybe he's just tired

from all the work he's been doing. When he gets home and his *bauch* starts growling this evening, he'll probably be really *hallich* he has a plate of *kuchen* all to himself."

"He won't share them with his wife?"

"*Neh*. He isn't married. Josiah lives alone right now."

"That's sad." Will hugged his aunt's legs. "I'm *hallich* I get to live here and help you until my *mamm* gets home."

"I'm *hallich*, too," Anke agreed, so touched by the child's sentiment that even as she was saying how happy she was, she had to wipe a tear from the corner of her eye.

Josiah knew that Anke had sensed the change in his attitude toward her and Will because he'd seen the way she'd set her jaw after he'd barely mumbled *denki* when Will had given him the plate of cookies he'd made.

In contrast with Anke's stony countenance, the child's expression was one of perplexed sweetness. Josiah knew Will looked up to him and the boy was undoubtedly confused by his sudden indifference. He so regretted offending Anke and hurting the boy's feelings that he'd almost returned to the *daadi haus* to apologize. But how would he excuse his behavior? He couldn't very well have said, *I'm concerned that if I continue being friendly with you, I might be ostracized. And not just me, but my* bruder *and his wife, too.* No, that would only hurt Anke and Will further. It was better to pull back without any explanation.

On the way home Josiah stopped at the smaller of the town's two grocery stores because its deli department offered premade meals. While not nearly as delicious as homemade food, they were a lot tastier than anything Josiah could have made for himself, but they were costlier, too. *What would I have done if Anke hadn't given me the job repairing the* daadi haus? he ruminated as he stood in line, still feeling guilty about his behavior. *I would barely be able to afford to eat butter and noodles every night.*

While he was thinking, someone behind him tapped his shoulder. He turned around to see Iddo Stoll, New Hope's deacon, standing behind him. "Are you in line for the bachelors' special?" he asked, gesturing toward the glass display case of heated, precooked food.

Josiah laughed. "*Jah.* I'm buying supper."

"I am, too. My wife, Almeda, is out of town, so I've got to hunt and forage until she returns from visiting her *schweschder* in Serenity Ridge," Iddo joked.

"How long is that?"

"She's coming back tomorrow. And to be honest, she had prepared four days' worth of meals before she left." The older man patted his stomach. "But I doubled up on yesterday's supper so here I am now."

"Well, I'd recommend the beef stroganoff over the *hinkel*," Josiah suggested. "By this time of evening, the *hinkel* is a little dried out from sitting beneath that warming light."

"Sounds like you've been getting your food here often. No one has hosted you for supper yet? That surprises me. Usually the *leit* in New Hope are a little more welcoming."

Josiah didn't want to mention that he'd been too busy working on Anke's *daadi haus* to really connect with any of the people from the district during the week. "Oh, the *leit* have been very welcoming—a group of them invited me to go snowshoeing with them. And one of the *weibsleit* brought me Long John Rolls."

The deacon raised an eyebrow. "Honor Bawell?"

"Jah." Josiah was perplexed by how he'd guessed.

"She brought me some, too, in Almeda's absence." He stroked his beard thoughtfully. "It was very kind of her and I appreciated the gesture…a lot more than I appreciated the taste."

Josiah had to laugh at that; he'd been so hungry he'd eaten two of the donuts the first night, just to keep his stomach from growling. But after he had finished them, his stomach made even more unsettling noises, so he'd broken the rolls in pieces and fed them to the chickens. "I'm surprised you didn't like them—Victor's *hinkel* gobbled them up."

"*Hinkel* eat bugs, so that's not saying much." The deacon smiled. "Since we're both on our own, why don't we eat our meals at my *haus*? It's not more than a mile and a half from here."

Josiah had been planning to make more progress on Victor and Laura's kitchen floor that night. He was also nervous that the deacon might question him about his work on Anke's *daadi haus*. But he knew it would have been rude to turn the deacon down, so he accepted. And it turned out that he was glad he did—he enjoyed getting to know Iddo and learning more about the New Hope district's history.

"I wish I would have remembered to get dessert," Iddo said after they'd finished their meals and he was making decaf coffee.

"I happen to have snickerdoodle *kuchen* in the buggy. We might have to wait until they thaw out a little, but I can go get them if you want me to?"

"Honor didn't make them, too, did she?"

"Neh." Josiah hesitated before he added, "They're from Anke."

"In that case, bring them in!"

The men finished off the plate of cookies long before they'd drunk their coffee. Iddo leaned back in his chair with a contented sigh. "I'd been hankering for something sweet. Almeda didn't leave me any dessert—she's trying to help me lose weight. So you'll have to tell Anke those *kuchen* hit the spot."

"Jah, they did," Josiah said noncommittally, since he didn't want to agree he'd pass along the deacon's compliment to Anke and Will. It might encourage them.

"How is the work coming on her *daadi haus*?"

"Fine. I should be done by the end of next week," Josiah said. Even though he knew the deacon had told Anke's family it wasn't a violation of the *Ordnung* for her to take care of Will, that didn't necessarily mean Iddo agreed with her decision. So Josiah quickly explained, "I wouldn't have taken the job, except I can't install fences in this weather."

"Well, then, I'm *hallich* that it's working out, for both your sakes. Almeda and I were praying someone would help her." Iddo looked Josiah squarely in the eye. "We knew that the work wouldn't be easy and it would take a strong man to do it."

Josiah immediately recognized what the deacon meant. Although he was being careful not to say anything that might seem to disparage the members of his district, Iddo was indicating he thought it was weak of them not to help Anke. He was acknowledging that he understood it took a man of strong character to associate with her by repairing the *daadi haus*. But Iddo was wrong about Josiah; he'd been cowardly. He'd been so afraid of how people would judge him that he hadn't really spoken his mind or stood up for Anke when he had the opportunity.

"I—I don't know if I'm as strong as you think I am," Josiah confessed.

"Your *bruder* told me in confidence what happened in Illinois," Iddo replied bluntly. "You're stronger than *you* think you are."

As the deacon raised his cup to his mouth and took a long pull of coffee, Josiah rubbed his eyes with his palms, simultaneously embarrassed and relieved that Iddo knew about the incident at the golf course. Mostly, he felt grateful that the deacon clearly wasn't judging him for what he'd done or making assumptions about his commitment to their Amish faith and lifestyle.

He also felt even more ashamed because *he* hadn't supported Anke in a similar manner. But that was about to change.

"*Neh*, I'm weak," Josiah insisted. "But *Gott* in me is strong and He'll help me repair what needs repairing."

On Saturday morning, Anke was surprised when Josiah knocked on the door half an hour earlier than usual. "I'll open it," Will volunteered.

"You haven't finished your breakfast yet. Your *oier* will get cold. I'll let Josiah in." The fact of the matter was that Anke didn't want Josiah's crankiness to affect Will's mood. The child was so excited about the prospect of seeing his cousins after lunch that he'd woken up at first light and asked her if it was almost time to go say he was sorry to his aunt for jumping on her couch. *If only we adults were that eager to apologize*, she thought ruefully as she opened the door for Josiah.

"*Gudermariye*, Anke. I'm sorry I'm early but I wanted to give something to Will before I got started working on the bedroom floor. I brought something for you, too." He reached into his pocket and pulled out a handful of fat batteries. "I noticed you've only been using the kerosene lamp lately, so I figured you might need these."

"That's thoughtful, but I'm going to town after lunch today, so I planned to pick up fresh batteries then."

"But I want you to have them as a small token of my appreciation for all the meals you've made for me. Including the *kuchen* you and Will baked yesterday. I shared them with the deacon last evening and he said to tell you they were *appenditlich*—and I agree."

As Josiah studied her, his reddish eyebrows nearly touched in the middle of his forehead and she realized he was anxiously awaiting her reply. It was clear he wasn't just offering her batteries; he was offering an apology for how he'd behaved the previous day. "*Denki.* That's a lovely gesture." As she took the batteries, her fingertips brushed his calloused palm, sending a shiver up her arm and down her spine.

"I finished my *oier*," Will announced as he came around from behind her. "Hi, Josiah. Did you know I'm going to see my *gschwischderkinner* after lunch?"

"I hope you have *schpass.*"

"Does that mean a snack?"

Josiah's curls seemed to bounce when he laughed. "*Neh.* It means fun."

"Oh, I'll have lots and lots of *schpass.*"

"I brought you something." Josiah held out two mason jars. One was empty and the other was filled with long screws.

Will reached for the jars. "Is this so I can build something?"

"*Neh.* This is so you will know how many days until your *mamm* is better and *kummes* home. You won't even have to ask your *ant* Anke." Josiah showed Will that he'd put forty-two screws, one for each day Clara was expected to be gone, into the jar. He explained that each evening before he went to bed, Will could take one of the screws from the clear mason jar and put it into the blue mason jar. "When you run out of screws in the clear jar, that's when your *mamm* will come home."

"But the blue jar doesn't have any screws in it at all." Will looked upset.

"You're right. How many nights have you been here?"

The boy glanced at Anke. "Five," she said. "Do you need me to help you count them out?"

"*Jah.* I can only count in *Englisch*," he replied.

Anke couldn't stop smiling. How she felt reminded her of the day her father had hung the swing in the tree for Clara. Her mother was delighted to see her young daughter enjoying herself so much. At the time, Anke was almost courting age and she never forgot that her mother had told her, *The way to a man's heart might be through his* bauch, *but the way to a woman's heart is through her* kind.

Now Anke knew exactly what she'd meant. Not that she thought Will was her child or that Josiah was trying to win her heart. But what he did for her nephew was so sweet she hummed her way through the morning.

For lunch she used the rest of the leftovers to make a "haystack casserole" and she was pleased when Josiah joined her and Will for lunch. The boy could hardly sit still and he practically inhaled his food.

"Slow down, Will," she told him. "There's no sense in hurrying—you're still going to have to wait for me to finish before we go next door."

After finishing what was on his plate, Will chatted away, informing Josiah, "*Ant* Anke's going to bring me some books from the library. She's going to teach me to read by myself. Not just the alphabet. Whole words—" He stopped suddenly and put a finger to his lips as if Josiah had been the one speaking, not him. "I hear *Onkel* Ernest's buggy!" he exclaimed.

Anke hadn't heard anything. "Are you sure? He usually doesn't get home from work for half an hour."

"Can I be 'scused to go look out the window?"

"Okay," Anke allowed. When he'd left the room, she said to Josiah, "I'm surprised your ears haven't fallen off yet. I'm sorry he's so talkative—he's just excited about seeing his *gschwischderkinner*. But if you're tired of listening to him, please feel free to tell him it's time to be quiet."

"I don't mind. The more he talks, the less he eats and the more there is for me," he joked. Or maybe he wasn't joking; he'd had three helpings of casserole and showed no signs of slowing down.

"We have *kuchen* for des—"

Anke was interrupted by Will wailing, "Where are they going?"

"Excuse me," she said, rising to go find out what Will was talking about, but he'd already returned to the room, a look of utter rejection on his face. "Did you see *Ant* Velda and the *kinner* go somewhere with *Onkel* Ernest?"

"*Neh*. They—they—they—" Will was obviously trying not to cry in front of Josiah.

"Take a deep breath," Anke instructed, giving him time to regain his composure. "That's right. Now, tell me what's wrong."

"They all got into a buggy and they went down the driveway."

Anke couldn't figure out what had happened. "Are you sure it wasn't *Onkel* Ernest's buggy? They all look similar."

"*Neh*. The *gaul* wasn't Star. It was kind of yellow."

Yellow? Anke wondered, trying to picture who owned a pale-colored horse in their district.

"Do you mean tan? Like this color?" Josiah asked Will, touching the table.

"*Jah*. And it had black legs up to its knees. Like socks."

"That was the Harnish *familye*'s buggy," Anke uttered.

"Keith Harnish?" Josiah asked.

"*Neh*. His *bruder* Saul. His wife, Ruth, is friends with Velda and they have two *kinner*, Eileen and Phineas, around the twins' age," she explained. "I don't know where they went, but don't worry, Will. I'm sure they'll be back soon."

But Anke was the one who was worried. It wasn't like her sister-in-law to go somewhere with all the children on a Saturday. *I hope none of the* kinner *is ill and they aren't on their way to the doctor*, she fretted. But then she told herself, *That can't be it—Velda would have told me. Besides, how would Ruth have known Velda needed a ride? They must have prear-*

ranged this trip to wherever they're going. Otherwise, Velda would have let her know, because she would have had to give Anke her grocery list so Anke could do her shopping for her. She silently asked the Lord to keep Velda and the children safe and healthy.

After Josiah resumed his work on the bedroom floor and Anke had cleaned up the kitchen, she played a card-matching game with Will. She was still so distracted by wondering where Velda was that her nephew matched five times as many cards as she did.

"Do you hear that?" Will asked, halfway through their second game. He hopped down from the kitchen chair and ran into the living room. A moment later he returned, his shoulders slumped. "It was only *Onkel* Ernest."

They finished playing the game and then Anke laid the cards out side by side on the table again. "This time, you get to see how long it takes you to find all the pairs yourself—no peeking. I'm going to go next door to ask your *onkel* if he knows where everybody went."

Before leaving, Anke stuck her head in the bedroom to let Josiah know she'd be right back.

"You want me to play cards with Will?" he volunteered.

"*Neh*. He's fine by himself. Please keep

doing what you're doing. I just wanted you to know where I was. I'll only be a minute."

She dashed across the lawn and into the house. "Is everything okay?" she breathlessly asked Ernest when she found him the kitchen.

He set down the glass of milk he'd just poured for himself. "Hi, Anke. Everything's fine as far as I know. Why?"

"Because I think Velda and the *kinner* went somewhere with Ruth Harnish in her buggy. I thought there might be an emergency."

Her brother put the glass bottle of milk into the fridge and then turned and scratched his bearded chin. Sometimes his slow, thoughtful responses were comforting. Other times, they drove Anke to distraction. "*Neh*, not as far as I know," he said. "She told me last night they were going to the market together. Then the *kinner* were going to play for a few hours at Ruth's *haus*. Didn't she mention it to you?"

"*Neh*," Anke spat out the word as if it was bitter on her tongue. "She didn't tell me. Apparently, she's not speaking to me at all."

Ernest shook his head. "I doubt that's true. Why wouldn't she be speaking to you at all?"

"Didn't she tell you about what happened the other day?"

"She said the *kinner* were misbehaving and she'd asked you to take Will home."

As calmly as she could, Anke relayed the entire story of what had happened, including what Will had told her about the illustration of a superhero cat wearing a cape like in the library book Velda had chosen for her children.

"Are you sure?" Ernest asked. "Velda is usually very careful about what the children read and look at."

Anke closed her eyes and let her breath out through her nose in a huff. She understood why her brother would be careful about jumping to conclusions, especially involving his wife. But it irritated her that he couldn't see how Velda was behaving. "I'll go get the book and we can take a look at it," she offered.

She went into the living room, found the book and brought it back. Maybe it was misplaced, but Anke had so much trust that Will had been telling her the truth that she didn't even need to open it to the page that contained the letter *C*. She simply handed her brother the book and watched his face as he flipped to the illustration in question. He shook his head, his mouth settling into a grim line.

"I'll speak with Velda," he said. "I'm sorry, Anke."

You're not the one who should be sorry, she thought. But after an urgent prayer for God to help her control her tongue, she replied, "I'm sure that when Velda understands what really happened, she'll remedy the situation right away."

At least, Anke hoped she would—for the children's sake.

Realizing he'd left a piece of equipment he needed on the porch, Josiah came out of the bedroom where he'd been working to retrieve it. Will must have heard the front door open because he came sailing into the room before Josiah had even stepped outside.

"Oh. I thought *Ant* Anke was back." His disappointment was almost palpable.

"*Neh*. But she should be here any second."

"Could you help me get a glass from the cupboard, please? I'm thirsty. And I can't stand on a chair to reach it—chairs are only for sitting on."

Josiah grinned; Anke's instructions obviously were sinking in. "Have you ever used a stepladder?"

"What's a stepladder?"

"It's a short ladder that carpenters use if they can't reach something by stretching."

Will shook his head. "*Neh*. I never used a stepladder. Just a ladder for climbing a slide."

"Would you like to use my stepladder to get a glass from the cupboard?"

"Jah." He jiggled his head up and down, so Josiah retrieved the ladder from the bedroom.

Setting it up in front of the sink, he cautioned, "Before you step on this, it's very, very important that you remember you're not allowed to use it without an adult like me around."

"I know. You have to say I can use it first."

"Right. Okay, I'll hold it steady and you can climb up."

The boy scaled the ladder quickly. When he reached the third step, he turned around. "I'm almost as tall as you," he said, even though his head barely came up to Josiah's chin.

"Almost. But every carpenter knows when he uses a ladder he's supposed to pay attention to what's in front of him, not what's behind. So turn around and open the cupboard."

Will retrieved a glass and handed it to Josiah. Then he backed down the ladder. "That was *schpass*," he said as he jumped off the bottom rung. Josiah folded the ladder, but Will protested, "I need to use it again so I can turn the faucet on."

"Neh, one climb per day," Josiah said. "I'll fill your glass for you."

As the boy was chugging down his water, the front door opened. "I'm back," Anke called. Right away, Josiah recognized the note of false cheerfulness in her voice. When she came into the kitchen and saw him there with her nephew, she said to Will, "Uh-oh. Did you disturb Josiah when he was working?"

"Neh," Josiah quickly answered for him. "I let him use my stepladder to get a glass since he didn't want to climb on the furniture. But don't worry—he knows he isn't allowed to use the ladder without me here to help him up and down."

This time, the cheerfulness in Anke's voice was genuine. "Wow, that's really nice of Josiah to share his ladder with you, Will. Isn't it?"

"Jah. I was as high as him," Will replied. "Where did *Onkel* Ernest say everybody went?"

"Well, because they didn't know we were coming over to see them after lunch, they all went shopping."

Josiah figured there was more to the story than Anke was letting on, but it wasn't any of his business, so he excused himself and picked up the stepladder. As he was leaving the room, he heard Will ask, "Are they coming back soon?"

"Neh. They…had some other places to go."

"After they go other places, can I play with them?"

"It will be too dark outside by then. But guess what you and I are going to do? We're going to go for a ride in the buggy. Won't that be *schpass*?"

Josiah quickly closed the bedroom door behind him so he wouldn't feel so sad when he heard the boy's disappointed reply.

Chapter Eight

Anke hoped Velda would come over and speak to her on Saturday evening, after Will had gone to bed. She even set the light in the window, so Velda would know she was still awake, but where it wouldn't shine in Will's eyes and disturb his sleep.

Not that he'd had any trouble dropping off; the day had been emotionally exhausting for the child. First, he'd gotten all wound up in anticipation of seeing his cousins, only to have his hopes dashed when they went to Ruth's house without him. Anke had been relieved that he'd perked up again when she took him to the store in the buggy. After that, they stopped at the library, where she'd checked out the maximum number of children's picture books permitted.

Their final stop was the wool shop because

Anke wanted to buy yarn to knit a warmer sweater for her nephew. That was when his mood took a downturn. *That was really my fault*, Anke thought as she rocked in front of the fire. *I shouldn't have told him he could choose the color.* Rather, she should have shown him which colors were acceptable, and then allowed him to choose from among them.

Instead, she'd made the mistake of saying he could choose any color he wanted, the way she would have told Micah or Millie or Asher. But that was only because they would have known they weren't allowed to choose orange, the way Will did. Then she had to tell him no, orange wasn't permitted. He'd burst into tears, drawing the attention of two women from her district who'd exchanged looks that Anke took as criticism.

It was my fault, she told herself again as she relived the scenario in her mind. *I got his hopes up and then pulled the carpet out from under him—and he'd already experienced that once today.* She could almost cry, just thinking about how when they'd arrived home, she'd suggested he look at a book while she made supper. By that time, Josiah had already left for the day. The *daadi haus* seemed so still and quiet that Anke popped her head into the living room to make sure Will hadn't fallen asleep while he was reading. Instead, she found him standing at the window; he'd been watching for Velda and the children to return.

"Will, it's almost supper time," she'd said. "Even if your *gschwischderkinner kumme* home, they won't be able to play. They'll have to go inside and eat." But he'd insisted on staying there, even after the sky grew dark.

"Why didn't Asher and Millie and Micah and Charity and *Ant* Velda *kumme* home yet?" he'd asked after they'd eaten supper and she'd read him three of his library books.

"Maybe they did *kumme*, but you didn't hear them."

"*Neh.* I have really *gut* ears. I didn't hear the buggy *kumme* up the driveway."

Anke knew he was right; he would have heard them. But she couldn't tell him what she really thought: that they'd come home *before* Anke and Will did, but Velda didn't want the two of them to know. So she'd kept everyone inside.

Now she wondered, *Why would she be so stubborn as to refuse the* kinner *to play together? Doesn't she realize she's punishing them as much as she's punishing Will?*

Whatever reason Velda had for still avoiding them, Anke hoped she got over it by tomorrow morning. She wanted to settle their differences so she and Will could join her brother's family for home worship on Sunday morning.

She finally turned out the light and crawled into bed. *Has it only been six nights that Will's been here?* she thought. It felt a lot longer than that. Yet in some ways, it also felt as if the time was passing too quickly. She already felt lonely when she imagined Will leaving.

That's not going to happen for over a month, she reminded herself. *And I've got a jar of screws to prove it.* Anke smiled when she recalled how happy Will was to take one of them out of the clear jar and drop it into the blue jar before he went to bed this evening. It even seemed to make him happier than looking at the photo of Clara.

The screw jars were such a gut *idea. Josiah really has a way with* kinner. *He'll make a* wunderbaar daed *someday,* she mused. For the briefest moment, as she pictured Josiah and his wife, along with their brood of curly red-headed children, Anke felt a wistfulness she'd never experienced before now.

That's lappich *of me to feel this way. I don't want a husband or* kinner. *Right now I've got my hands full taking care of Will,* she thought. And if the Lord answered Anke's prayers, Clara would return to New Hope and she and her son would stay there for good. *She'll need my help raising him, which I'll be overjoyed to do. And even if that doesn't happen, Velda and Ernest will still need me to help them with their kinner.*

No, Anke didn't want a family of her own—she loved the family she already had. But as she drifted off to sleep, she caught herself wishing that Velda would go visit her relatives in Canada and leave Will's cousins behind so the children could play together whenever they wanted.

On Sunday morning as Josiah directed his horse toward the park near the gorge, he reflected on what a meaningful time of worship he'd had with the Nisley family. They'd read a passage in Scripture from the Sermon on the Mount and they'd sung a couple of his favorite contemporary hymns together. Not to mention, Hope and her daughters had prepared leftovers for lunch that were far more flavorful than the best meal he'd bought from the supermarket.

Between eating with Iddo the other night and worshipping with the Nisleys this morning, Josiah was beginning to feel a lot more comfortable in New Hope. However, he wished he didn't have to go snowshoeing with the other single people in the district this afternoon. Actually, he was looking forward to going snowshoeing for the first time—especially since today was a good fifteen degrees warmer than it had been all week—but he wished he didn't have to go with Keith and Honor.

Josiah found it difficult to believe that only a couple of days ago, he was afraid of being excluded from his peer group, but now he was regretting that they'd included him. It wasn't that he was ungrateful or that he meant to be unkind, but he wasn't receptive to Honor's flirtations or to Keith's comments about Anke.

Anke. If Josiah had his way, he'd prefer to spend the day with her and Will. As he turned down the last road before the park, Josiah imagined him and Anke taking her nephew sledding or skating. Then he found himself imagining what it would be like to go out with Anke alone—to take her out to a restaurant or for a buggy ride, the way he might do if they were courting.

I can't let myself get carried away, he thought. *Just because I'm no longer concerned if the* leit *in New Hope will judge me for working on Anke's* daadi haus *doesn't mean I'd want to be her suitor. Besides, she's too wrapped up in caring for her nephew.*

Although Josiah admired Anke's dedication to supporting her sister, there was something about it that reminded him of how loyal Jana had been to her family, too. Of course, being committed to one's family wasn't just admirable—it was essential, as far as Josiah was concerned. However, in Jana's case, she was so loyal to her family that she couldn't even consider that her father might have been mistaken or that her brother could have done something wrong. Instead, she'd suspected one of *Josiah's* family members had been drinking. While he had no good reason to believe that Anke would act in a similar manner, there was something about her relationship with Clara that made him wary anyway.

If I learned anything from courting Jana, it's that I'll spare myself a world of hurt by staying single, he thought as he spied several other buggies in the parking lot. *Now, if I can only get that message across to Honor, I might actually have a pleasant afternoon.*

Maybe Velda is waiting for me to kumme *to her*, Anke thought as she dried the last of the lunch dishes. Since her sister-in-law hadn't dropped in to speak about what had happened, Anke had assumed Velda didn't want her and Will coming to their home worship service earlier that morning. She realized that may have been an incorrect assumption, but she wasn't going to take any chances of being turned away at the door and crushing her nephew's hopes once again.

So Anke had conducted her own home worship service with Will. First, she'd read to him from the Bible and then she'd taught him the simple *Englisch* song "Jesus Loves the Little Children."

After they'd sung the line about all children being precious in His sight, Will had asked, "Does Jesus love *kinner* like me as much as He loves Amish *kinner* like Asher and Millie and Micah and Charity?"

"*Jah*, every bit as much," Anke had answered unequivocally. "And I love you every bit as much as I love your *gschwischderkinner*, too."

"Can I play with them today?"

"I'm not sure. The Sabbath is a day of rest, so they might have to stay inside and take long naps." Anke had known how weak her excuse sounded and she'd expected Will to ask a stream of questions, but he hadn't.

"Maybe when they wake up, *Ant* Velda will let them *kumme* out to play," he'd said, but he didn't sound convinced.

Now as Anke returned the clean lunch plates to the cupboard, she thought, *It's a lot warmer outside today. Maybe I can take Will for a walk—I could pull him on the sled.*

She went into the living room to find him bent over a picture book on his lap, his blond head like a little ball of sunshine. Sitting in the big chair, the boy appeared even smaller than usual; he appeared out of place. And suddenly Anke felt a surge of anger at her sister-in-law. *If it weren't for Velda, Will would be playing with the other* kinner, *not reading alone in an* eldre's *chair.*

She cleared her voice and asked, "How would you like it if we went outside and I gave you a ride on the sled?"

Will shrugged. "I don't know."

"It's a lot warmer out today and I'll put a blanket over you so you won't get cold," she assured him. "I can't gallop as fast as Star can, but I can trot nice and steady. It'll be *schpass*."

"Okay." His tone was one of resignation, not excitement.

As they were putting on their coats and hats, Anke heard the unmistakable sound of an approaching buggy and her stomach dropped. *Please*, Gott, *let that be Josiah*, she prayed. There wasn't any reason for the carpenter to drop by the *daadi haus* today, but he was the only person Anke could imagine visiting them. Whoever else may have arrived would be coming to see Ernest's family—and that meant

Will would likely be excluded from playing with the children again.

The boy had heard the buggy, too, and he darted to the window, one sneaker on, one off. "Somebody's here!" he shouted.

"It's probably one of the *weibsleit* from *kurrich* coming to see your *ant* Velda," Anke told him. "*Kumme* away from the window—it's not polite to stare."

Will reluctantly obeyed, dragging himself over to where Anke was holding out his sneaker for him. *These shoes aren't warm enough for him to go tromping through the snow—it's a* gut *thing I'm pulling him on the sled.*

When she handed him his hat, he said, "I can't wear that. It's got orange on it. Orange is too bright and it makes me get attention."

He was more or less repeating what Anke had told him about the yarn he'd chosen yesterday—that the Amish considered it prideful to draw attention to oneself by wearing bright colors. "I think it would be okay for you to wear your hat since you aren't wearing it because it's bright. You're wearing it to keep warm."

"Can't I just wear my hood?"

Anke vacillated. "Okay. But I'll bring your hat with us, just in case—" She stopped talking when she heard footsteps on the porch.

Will had heard them, too, and he tried to open the door, but he couldn't get a grip on the knob because he was wearing mittens. Anke was almost as excited as he was to see who was there. She gently nudged him out of her way. "Here, I'll open it."

"They're home, *Daed*!" a blonde girl even littler than Will shouted. It was Sovilla Lehman—Arleta's four-year-old daughter. Standing at the bottom of the stairs was Noah, Arleta's husband.

"Hello, Anke. I hope we're not interrupting your naps?" he asked.

"Not at all. We were just getting ready to go outside."

Anke was about to introduce her nephew to Sovilla and Noah, but he'd already squeezed past her and announced, "Hi, I'm Will."

"I'm Sovilla. Can I see inside your *haus*?"

"*Neh*, Sovilla," Noah forbade his daughter. For one halting second, Anke was afraid he didn't want her going into the house because an *Englischer* lived in it. But then he added, "You weren't invited and it's not polite to invite yourself."

"She's *wilkom* to go in. Will, show Sovilla the living room and kitchen." Anke moved aside, allowing the little girl to enter. Then she stepped onto the porch and pulled the door almost shut behind her so the heat wouldn't escape. "I'd invite you to look around, too, but it's so small in there I'm not sure everyone would fit."

Noah chuckled. "That's okay. I don't plan to stay. We just stopped by to ask if Will wanted to go sledding with us over by the *schul*. Arleta couldn't *kumme*—she has a *koppweh*."

"I'm sorry to hear that. I hope she feels better soon." While Anke appreciated the invitation to go sledding, she was surprised Noah had invited her to go with him without Arleta present. It didn't seem appropriate for her to accompany a married man on an outing without his wife, but Anke didn't know how to express that or what other excuse to give for declining.

"I sense Arleta will feel much better once she's had some rest. She said she thought you might need a little peace and quiet for yourself, too. She gave me a very firm reminder to tell you I promise not to allow the *kinner* to go down the hill too quickly."

Relieved to realize Noah wasn't inviting *her* to go sledding with him and the children, Anke laughed. "I trust you," she said. "My only concern is that Will doesn't have decent boots. But I suppose he'll be okay if he puts on another pair of socks."

"That should help. And if he's anything like Sovilla, he'll want me to give him a ride up the hill on the sled, instead of walking through the snow himself."

"In that case, maybe I should give *you* another pair of socks," Anke joked. Her heart felt ten pounds lighter. And when she told Will he got to go sledding with his new friend, his elated reaction made her feel as if her heart might float away altogether.

For the duration of their snowshoeing excursion, Josiah had managed to avoid engaging in any conversation with Keith except friendly, superficial small talk. Nor had he fallen behind the others and gotten stuck alone with Honor. Instead, he'd kept pace with two other young men, Ervin and Jacob. They'd given him a few pointers about how to dig his toes into the snow as he was going uphill, but other than that, he was surprised at how naturally easy it was to transverse the snowy terrain.

"*Denki* for inviting me to *kumme* with you," he said at the end of their hike. The group was crossing the final field together, at a slower, leisurely pace. "It's really beautiful here and I felt like I got a *gut* workout."

"*Jah,*" Keith agreed. "All this exercise has made me *hungerich*. I wish there were someplace nearby where we could get a bite to eat, don't you, Glenda?"

"You mean like my *familye*'s restaurant, don't you?" she said. Her parents owned Millers' Restaurant.

"I hadn't thought of that," Keith said, even though he clearly had. "But now that you mention it…sure, I guess I could stop there, since it's on my way home."

Josiah couldn't keep the disbelief from his tone when he asked, "Your *familye*'s restaurant is open on the Sabbath?"

"Only for pleasure, not for business. That's why Keith dropped his very obvious hint—he knows my *mamm* sometimes allows my siblings and me to bring our friends there to eat *Samschdaag's* leftovers," Glenda explained.

"Oh. That makes sense. For a minute though, I was thinking, *Whoa—the* leit *in New Hope conduct business on* Sundaag? *That's a lot different than in the district I came from,*" Josiah admitted. "I should have known better."

"Ha!" Keith guffawed. "Of *course* we don't conduct business on a *Sundaag.* Most of us don't associate with *Englisch* alcoholics, either…or with other people who do."

Josiah's pulse thumped in his ears. *How does Keith know about what happened at the golf course in Illinois?* he wondered. But then he realized that Keith was actually referring to Clara. As usual, he had found a way to bring up the topic of Anke's decision to care for Will. Josiah decided not to take the bait and kept tramping toward the parking lot as if he hadn't heard Keith's remark.

"Who else is going to the restaurant?" Honor asked. Everyone said they'd go, except for Josiah, who remained silent. So Honor pressed him, questioning, "How about you, Josiah? Are you coming, too?"

"*Denki*, but *neh*. Not this time."

"But you must be *hungerich*, aren't you? Just *kumme* and hang out with us for a little while. The food will be *appenditlich*."

Josiah appreciated being included, but he wished Honor would accept his decision without arguing. *Even Will has already learned that* neh *means* neh, *and he's only a* kinner, he thought. An *Englisch* one, at that. But Josiah realized she wasn't going to stop pestering him until he gave her a reason for not joining the group.

"*Jah*, I've heard *gut* things about Millers' Restaurant and I plan to eat there one day soon," he said, so he wouldn't offend Glenda. "But I'd like to spend part of the Sabbath resting in preparation for the long week I have ahead of me."

"Pfbt." Keith made a scoffing sound. "How much work can there be to do on Anke's *daadi haus* anyway? It's the size of a bread box. If I didn't know better, I'd think you were drawing the job out because you *enjoy* working for her."

"Actually, you'd be right. I *do* enjoy working for Anke," Josiah blurted out. Then, because he realized that it sounded as if he was interested in her romantically, he added, "She's been a *gut* employer. She pays me a generous salary and she's not unreasonable or demanding, the way some homeowners are."

"I'm sure that's true. She's always been very kind to everyone." Honor panted as she tried to keep up with them and simultaneously insert herself into their conversation. "But sometimes, she lets people take advantage of her *gut* nature."

Josiah stopped short. "You think I'm somehow taking advantage of Anke's *gut* nature?" he spoke louder than he intended. Or maybe his voice just rang out because they were in an open field.

"*Neh*, I didn't mean you, *lappich*." Honor playfully nudged his shoulder, setting him into motion again. "I meant her *schweschder* and her nephew. She loves Clara so much she allowed Will to live with her. And I think she spoils him. Like the other day when I came over and the three of you were sitting there eating chocolate *kuche* first thing in the morning."

So says the weibsmensch who'd stopped by at ten-thirty with Long John Rolls, Josiah thought, scanning the field. Another hundred yards and he'd be at his buggy—he lengthened his stride.

"Josiah was having breakfast with Anke and Will?" Keith questioned Honor.

"*Neh*, not breakfast." Jabbing both poles into the snow, Josiah came to a standstill. He was fed up. "I was taking a short break from work and Anke was thoughtful enough to offer me a piece of *kuche*. You're right, it was chocolate and Will and Anke had some, too. As for her spoiling him—only *Gott* can judge whether that's true. But from what I've overheard while I've been working, Anke constantly instructs and corrects the *bu*. She's doing her best to educate him about our lifestyle and customs. And she's trying to teach him about *Gott*'s love and forgiveness—she's modeling it for him, as well. Which, as I understand it, is something we're all called to do."

Josiah looked back and forth from Honor to Keith, almost daring them to contradict him. In his peripheral vision, he saw their peers shift their stances and Josiah regretted making them uncomfortable, but he felt this was something that he'd needed to express. In fact, he should have said it long ago.

When neither Keith nor Honor said anything else, Josiah yanked his poles from the snow. "As I said, I really enjoyed snowshoeing with everybody. I hope to join you again soon. But I'm tired now and I'm going home. See you later."

He'd advanced maybe fifteen yards when he overheard Faith giggle. "There's only one reason a *mann* defends a *weibsmensch* like that— he must really like her. He probably wants to be her suitor."

Josiah was tempted to turn around and tell her she couldn't be more wrong. But the fact was, she may have been more right than he wanted to admit.

It was almost three thirty and Anke knew that at any minute Noah would bring Will home. As delighted as she was to know he was out having a fun time with another child close to his age, for the past two hours Anke had felt an overwhelming sense of loneliness for the boy. She was aware it wasn't because he'd left for the afternoon—it was because she knew it was a foretaste of how she'd feel once Clara got out of the recovery program and took him back to Portland with her. *That day hasn't* kumme *yet. I don't know what* Gott *has in store for us*, she reminded herself. Then she'd spent the next half an hour praying for her sister; in particular, she'd asked the Lord to urge her to return to New Hope and to her family for good.

Anke had also asked God to help change her own attitude toward Velda. She'd been wrestling with resentment because her sister-in-law was apparently still refusing to allow Will to come to the house, even though Asher was as responsible for their behavior as Will had been. *Maybe she's not being stubborn*, Anke thought. *Maybe she's ill.*

Then again, yesterday she'd been worried that something had happened to Velda or the children—and they'd been fine. *Neh, she's deliberately distancing herself and her* fami- lye *from us.* It seemed so immature. So spiteful. Almost cruel. The more Anke dwelled on it, the worse Velda's behavior seemed to her and the angrier she became. *So much for enjoying an afternoon to myself*, she thought. The house may have been quiet, but Anke's thoughts were hardly peaceful. Suddenly, she recalled the verse that began "Blessed *are* the peacemakers…"

Anke knew that for her own good, as well

as for Velda's and the children's, she had to be the one to go make peace with her sister-in-law. And she had to do it quickly, before Noah returned with Will. She pulled on her coat and dashed across the yard. When she reached the porch, she knocked on the door, even though doing so really got her goat. A moment later, Velda opened it.

Her eyes were pink rimmed, there were three pins sticking out crookedly from her hair and she wasn't wearing a prayer *kapp*. "Are you ill?" Anke immediately asked.

Velda burst into tears. *"Neh."*

Alarmed, Anke put her arm around her and led her to the couch, where they sat down beside each other. "Then what's wrong? Did something happen to Ernest or the *kinner*?"

"Neh. They're all upstairs napping." Velda covered her face with her arm, crying as she spoke. "Or they're pretending to nap—they're probably afraid to *kumme* down. I've been so short-tempered. I even raised my voice to Charity this morning and made her cry. I feel *baremlich* about it…and about how I treated Will. And you. Oh, Anke—I'm so sorry!"

Velda continued to weep as she explained that she'd wanted to come over to apologize and to set things right. But she'd been too ashamed for blaming Will for being the one to suggest jumping on the couch. And because she was mortified about the book she'd allowed the children to check out of the library.

"It's okay," Anke comforted her. "Will is eager to apologize to *you* for jumping on your couch. He knows it's not acceptable behavior—and that he's not allowed to talk about superheroes with your *kinner*. As far as your checking out a book with a picture like that in it...you didn't know. It's not as if you did it on purpose."

"I *should* have known. I should have read it thoroughly first." Velda sobbed even harder. "I know it's prideful, but I feel like such a failure as a *mamm*."

"I understand you're upset, but I doubt that picture will have a lasting effect on your *kinner*. So you made one tiny oversight, but that's absolutely nothing compared to all the love and guidance and nurturing you've given your *kinner*."

"*Neh*, you *don't* understand," Velda insisted. "It's *not* a tiny oversight, don't you see?"

Anke shook her head, puzzled by why her sister-in-law was so upset. "I'm sorry, but I don't."

"Be-because for five years, I've listened to the pain in your *bruder*'s voice every single night when he's prayed for your *schweschder*," she explained. "I was so determined not to ever allow our *kinner* to be influenced by the *Englisch* because I couldn't stand the thought of Ernest bearing that kind of burden again…"

She cried so hard she had to stop speaking, but she didn't need to say anything else anyway. Anke understood now why she was so upset about the book and about Will visiting New Hope. As moved as she was by her sister-in-law's disclosure, Anke still didn't think it was fair to forbid the children to play with one another.

"*Denki* for sharing that with me, Velda," she said. "It helps me understand why you feel so strongly about protecting your *kinner*. And I respect your decision in the matter. But I really don't believe Will is going to negatively influence Millie and Micah and Asher. If anything, in the past week, I've seen how living here has positively influenced *him*."

She paused while Velda lifted her apron to her face and dried her eyes. But when her sister-in-law didn't say anything, Anke suggested, "What if one—or both—of us is always present when the *kinner* are together? What if we never let them out of sight or earshot like I had to do the other day? *Then* will you be more comfortable occasionally allowing them to play together?"

"I—I don't know," she said. "I need to talk to the Lord about it."

"That's a *gut* idea—but you'd better put on your prayer *kapp*, first."

Velda lifted her hands to pat her bare head. "Ach! What a mess I am," she uttered. "The house is, too. I'm going to pieces without you here."

Even though her sister-in-law's remark bordered on being a complaint, Anke understood it was Velda's way of saying she appreciated how much work Anke did, and she smiled to herself.

When she got back to the *daadi haus*, she was surprised to see it was almost four o'clock and Noah still hadn't returned with the children. *I've had enough peace and quiet for one day—now I want Will here*, she thought. *And it will be nice to have Josiah back again tomorrow, too.*

Closing her eyes, she pictured his curly locks and the dusting of freckles on his forehead. Then she reminisced about him bringing her batteries for the lamp and how she'd felt when her fingers had brushed his skin…

Her thoughts were interrupted when Noah's buggy came up the lane. *I shouldn't be thinking about such things anyway*, she told herself. Those were the kind of daydreams a woman had about her suitor, not about a man she hardly knew. Besides, she had her sister's child to focus on—and when he came in the door, she forgot about everything except his smile.

"Sovilla's *daed* is so strong. He walked up the hill with me riding on his shoulders and he pulled Sovilla on the sled at the same time! And he gave us big pushes down the hill. But he said they were only medium-fast because Sovilla's *mamm* didn't want us to go full speed," Will raved. Hardly pausing to take a breath, he asked, "Is it time for supper? I'm *hungerich*."

Anke laughed. "*Jah*, it's almost time to eat. We're having *supp*. While I'm heating it, I'd like you to take off your shoes and warm your toes in front of the fire. Your feet must be awfully cold."

"*Neh*. Only a little."

Noticing he had a knot in his laces, Anke helped him remove his sneakers. She pressed her hand to his toes and could feel they were cold even through two pairs of socks. Buying him a pair of boots was essential, especially if the weather stayed warm enough for him to go outside to play. But how would Anke get into town this week? She supposed she could pull Will on the sled. Or better yet, she could ask Josiah to borrow his buggy. *Then I could repay him by inviting him to stay for a nice supper*, she absentmindedly schemed before she realized her mind had drifted to romantic thoughts of Josiah again.

I can't believe I'm contriving ways to bribe him to spend more time with us, she thought as she went into the kitchen and began stirring the pot of soup. *It's completely* lecherich. *He has other things to do in the evening*.

"Someone's here!" Will yelled and by the time Anke entered the living room, he'd already opened the door.

"Hello, Will. Hi, Anke," Velda greeted them both and so did Asher, who was standing at her side.

Will apologized before he even said hello. "I'm sorry I jumped on the couch, *Ant* Velda. I won't do it ever, ever again. Furniture is for sitting on. And we don't believe in superheroes. Only *Gott*." Then he added, "Hi, Asher. I missed you."

Anke noticed he used the word *we* instead of *you* or *Amish people*. In the back of her mind, she wondered whether that meant he considered himself to be Amish, now, too. But she was more interested in hearing how Velda and Asher responded to Will's apology.

"Hi, Will. I missed you every day." Asher spread his arms and embraced his cousin. When he let go, he gazed up at Anke. "I told Will to jump on the couch. He didn't tell me to do it first."

Anke nodded. "*Jah*. I know. I imagine you're not going to jump on furniture again, either, are you?"

"*Neh*. Never."

"And I'm not going to jump to conclusions," Velda joked nervously, but the boys were too young to understand her pun. They looked at her blankly, so she crouched down by Will and said, "I'm sorry I thought you told Asher to jump on the couch. I made a mistake."

"It's okay." Will wrapped his arms around her neck, practically hanging on her. Anke was just about to tell him he needed to let go now, when he murmured, "You feel soft, *Ant* Velda. Just like my *mamm*."

Velda patted his back and stood up so he had to release his grasp, but Anke noticed her eyes were swimming with tears. "Would you two like to join us for leftovers?" Velda asked.

"I was just warming up a pot of *supp*, but we'd much rather have leftovers at your *haus* with all of you. Wouldn't we, Will?" Anke asked. But the boy was too preoccupied with putting his sneakers on to answer.

Chapter Nine

When Anke opened the door on Monday morning, Josiah could tell right away that she and Velda had reconciled their differences. Her eyes sparkled like spring grass after a fresh rain and her lips danced with a smile. But in case he had any doubt, Will came charging into the room and exclaimed, "Hi, Josiah. Guess what I did yesterday?" Without waiting for him to guess, the child said, "I went sledding with Sovilla and her *daed* on a big hill and then *Ant* Anke and I ate supper with Asher and Micah and Millie and Charity and *Onkel* Ernest and *Ant* Velda."

Will could have just said he'd eaten supper with his cousins and aunts and uncle, but Josiah recognized that the child considered each of his relatives so special, he had to list them by name. "That sounds like quite a *schpass* day."

"*Jah*. It was. And we got to have leftovers for supper—those are my favorite," Will said earnestly. Josiah caught Anke fighting a smile, obviously trying to contain her amusement.

"Would you like a cup of *kaffi*?" she asked Josiah.

"I probably shouldn't since I had two at breakfast, but I'd like one anyway. It's supposed to get to thirty-five degrees this afternoon, but it's still chilly out there this morning—a cup of *kaffi* will warm me up."

"You should take a seat by the stove," Anke suggested. "If you have the time to visit, I mean."

I'll take *the time if it means I get to bask in the glow of your smile*, Josiah thought dreamily. Anke's vivaciousness was so charming this morning it was almost making him dizzy. "I have a few minutes, sure," he said.

"You can sit in my chair," Will offered, as generous as always. He followed Anke into the kitchen. A second later, there was a loud scraping sound as Will dragged the chair into the living room and placed it next to where Josiah was sitting. The boy perched on it and asked, "Did you have a *schpass* day yesterday, too?"

"*Jah*, I did." He took the mug from Anke, who'd come back into the room. After giving it to him, she settled into the rocker.

"Was it more *schpass* than going sledding and eating leftovers?"

"Hmm. Probably not. But I did go snowshoeing."

"What's that?"

"It's when you wear special shoes that allow you to walk on the snow without sinking into it. And you use poles to help you move forward and to balance." Josiah sipped his coffee—it was nice and strong, even by Amish standards.

"Did you go with somebody?"

"Will, It's not polite to pry." Anke held a finger to her lips. Why had her smile suddenly disappeared? Was she that upset about her nephew's manners?

"That's okay. I don't mind telling him," Josiah said, and listed the name of each person who'd gone snowshoeing, just as Will had done.

"That's a lot of people."

"*Jah*. It was." Josiah addressed Anke. "Have you ever gone snowshoeing, Anke?"

"On occasion, *jah*." Her answer seemed a little curt and Josiah had no clue how to account for the sudden change in her mood.

"Did you enjoy it?"

"*Jah.*"

"Did you have leftovers when you were done snowshoeing?" Will wanted to know.

"Well, everybody else did. Glenda's *familye* owns a restaurant. It was closed because it was the Sabbath, but her *mamm* and *daed* allowed her to bring her friends there to eat."

"But not you?"

"*Neh.* I wasn't very *hungerich* yet. So I went home and ate a bowl of chili."

"What kind of restaurant was it?"

He's asking so many questions this morning—usually Anke would have told him he had to stop by now, Josiah thought. "It was an Amish restaurant."

"I never went to an Amish restaurant before. Sometimes my *mamm* takes me to a pizza restaurant. That's my favorite kind. But it's *Englisch.*"

Josiah was suddenly inspired. "Well, I'll tell you what. Since you like going out for pizza so much, when I finish making all the repairs I need to make on the *daadi haus*, I'll take you to a pizzeria to celebrate—but only if your *ant* Anke doesn't mind?" He raised his eyebrow at her.

"That's generous of you, but it's not necessary."

"But if you let me take you and Will out for

pizza, you'll get a break from making supper in that tiny kitchen of yours. Wouldn't that be nice?"

Will leaned over and whispered loudly to Josiah, "*Ant* Anke says when an *eldre* makes a decision, we aren't supposed to argue."

"Will, *kinner* are not supposed to tell *eldre* what to do, either!" Anke exclaimed.

Josiah couldn't help it; he burst out laughing. "He's right, though. I shouldn't twist your arm. If you'd rather not go, there's no pressure." *Even if I'd really like to take you and Will out*, he thought.

Anke hesitated before she answered. When Josiah had first started telling Will about how much fun he'd had snowshoeing with Honor and the others, Anke had felt an undeniable twinge of envy. She could envision Honor flirting with him and she'd wondered if he had felt flattered or had reciprocated her attention. She was so curious that she'd even allowed Will to ask Josiah more personal questions about his afternoon than she ordinarily would have permitted.

Then, when he'd mentioned taking the boy out for pizza, Anke had thought Josiah just meant he was going to take Will out alone, kind of as a male bonding experience. But now that she knew he wanted to take her, too, it felt a little awkward. Almost as if he was leading up to asking her to walk out with him. In which case, she'd have to say no. Because no matter if she *had* been playing with thoughts of what it would be like to have him as a suitor, she didn't have time for courting. Not now, when Will was here. And not in the future, either—Velda had already admitted she couldn't manage her household without Anke.

Or was she reading too much into his invitation? She supposed since the three of them had been eating meals together all along, it seemed only natural that Josiah would include Anke, too. She was the child's aunt and Josiah's friend; that was probably all there was to it. In any case, it was a gracious invitation and Anke decided to accept.

"*Denki.* You're right—it would be nice not to have to cook supper in such a tiny kitchen for one evening," she said.

"*Wunderbaar,*" Will and Josiah both exclaimed at the same time, making Anke laugh.

For the next few days, she felt as if she could hardly contain her happiness. She had reconciled with Velda, the children were allowed to play together, the repairs were progressing smoothly *and* she had a celebration of sorts to look forward to at the end of the week with Josiah and Will.

Denki, *Lord, for Your abundant provisions*, she prayed on Thursday morning when she knelt beside her bed. He had given her so many blessings she felt greedy asking for any more. But she had determined long ago that she would never stop requesting for the Lord to bring Clara home. So she added, *Please give my* schweschder *a deep desire to repent and return to us for* gut…*after she's completed her recovery program.*

Even as she rose from her knees, Anke realized the last part of her request was for her own benefit, as much as it was for Clara's. Yes, Anke wanted her sister to meet the requirements the judge had set for her. And yes, she wanted Clara to be free from her addiction to alcohol. But she also wanted her sister to remain in the recovery program so Anke could spend the full six weeks taking care of Will by herself.

Although she loved all of her nieces and nephews equally, Anke felt a special closeness with Will. Almost as if she was more like a mother to him than an aunt. Maybe that was because his mother wasn't always around, like Velda was. Or because Anke and Will lived in a separate house where she didn't have to divide her attention between multiple children. In any case, she wanted to make the most of every day with him.

"*Gudermariye, Ant Anke,*" he said, interrupting her thoughts. "Why were you looking at me?"

"Because I love you so much I like to look at you even when you're asleep. But I'm *hallich* you're awake because I need you to help me gather *oier* for breakfast."

"Is Josiah going to eat with us?"

"I don't know." Josiah had accepted Anke's invitation to have pancakes with her and Will yesterday morning, even though he'd already eaten breakfast at home. "Why?"

"Because I like it when he eats with us. My *daed* never ate with me before."

Anke caught her breath. She knew Will's father must have eaten with them all of the time. So it was clear what the boy was actually expressing was that he didn't *remember* his father eating with him. It was also clear that Will was associating Josiah with a father figure. *I don't know if that's* gut *for him*, Anke fretted.

But then Will added, "If Josiah is going to eat with us, we need to gather lots and lots of *oier* and then Asher and Micah and Millie and Charity and *Ant* Velda might not get any."

Anke chuckled and her fears about Will becoming too attached to Josiah quickly dissipated. "Josiah doesn't need *that* many *oier*. We'll be sure to leave plenty for your *ant* and *gschwischderkinner*."

"Even enough for Charity?" The day before, Will had been astounded to see the infant shoveling double fistfuls of scrambled eggs into her mouth.

"*Jah*. Even enough for Charity. Now hurry and go get dressed so Josiah doesn't think you're a *schlofkopp*." Anke teased, using the word for *sleepyhead*. *And I'd better brush my hair and wash my face so he doesn't think I look like something the cat dragged in*, she thought. And while she was at it, she decided to put on a fresh apron, too.

Josiah had only been working for half an hour when he realized he'd forgotten to bring the pneumatic drill he needed back to the *daadi haus* with him. He'd taken it home with him last night to drill pilot holes in the wood of the floor he was laying for Laura and Victor. He hoped Ernest had one he could borrow, otherwise, he'd have to go all the way back home to get it and that would slow his progress considerably.

Not that he was in any hurry to finish this project. He'd had such a pleasant week listening to Anke and Will talking, reading and laughing together as he worked. He always knew when Anke was baking; not just because of the delicious aromas that permeated the air, but also because he could hear her humming or singing to herself. When the treats had cooled, she'd allow Will to knock on the door to the bedroom and ask if he wanted to take a break and have a sweet with them. Of course, Josiah always said yes and he ate lunch with them, as well.

His experience of repairing the *daadi haus* this past week with Anke and Will nearby was similar to how Josiah had pictured his life would be after he married Jana. Except in a way, this was better because…well, because Anke wasn't going to betray him and devastate him the way Jana did. How could she? They weren't courting and he hadn't opened his heart to Anke.

But he *did* like being in her company. So he wasn't concerned if he didn't finish the repairs on Saturday as he'd projected he would do. However, he disliked making extra trips. Even if the temperature was a couple of degrees warmer than the day before, so much back and forth was hard on the horse. And in general, Josiah didn't relish traveling in *Englisch* traffic when the roads were wet or snowy.

But after Velda gave him permission, Josiah looked through Ernest's tools and equipment and didn't find the kind of drill he needed.

"I'm afraid I'm going to have to go home and get mine," he told Anke, who was hanging Will's socks in front of the woodstove while the boy was reading in his chair. She wrinkled her forehead and parted her lips as if she wanted to say something, yet she didn't. *Is she upset because I made such a* dumm *mistake?* Josiah wondered. "I'm sorry I forgot it. I know you're eager to have your own bedroom, so I can work a little later tonight to make up for lost time."

"*Neh*, there's no need to do that. I was just wondering…"

Josiah was intrigued. What could she be so hesitant to ask him? "Wondering what?" he prompted.

She held up a sock. "Will's feet keep getting wet when he plays outside because he only has sneakers to wear. Unfortunately, my sister-in-law gave her *buwe*'s boots away, so we don't have any hand-me-downs for him to use. I was wondering if he and I could go with you and we could swing by the shoe store in town?"

"*Jah*. It would be my pleasure." Josiah really meant it. "While you're getting your coat on, I'll go hitch the *gaul*."

"I'll help you!" Will scrambled for his coat and mittens.

"Josiah doesn't need your—" Anke started to say, but Josiah waved his hand to indicate it was fine if Will came with him.

In the barn, the boy stayed to the side, as he was told, and he listened intently while Josiah explained everything he was doing as he hitched the buggy to the horse. Josiah explained that his father had taught him the same way. "Once I was tall enough to fasten all the straps, it was my responsibility to hitch the horse and buggy every *Sundaag* before we went to *kurrich.*"

"Didn't you have *kurrich* in your *haus*?" Will was obviously unaware that last week was an off-Sunday.

"*Jah.* But every other *Sundaag,* we met at someone else's *haus.* Here in New Hope, every other *Sundaag,* we meet in our *kurrich* building."

As soon as the words were out of his mouth, Josiah wished he could take his explanation back. What if Anke hadn't been planning to bring him to church? He couldn't imagine *her* missing a service, but maybe she had arranged for a member of the Serenity Ridge district to watch him, since their church schedule was the opposite of New Hope's. *I'm such a* bobbelmoul, he lamented. But there was nothing he could do about it now; he'd have to mention his blunder to Anke later, when Will wasn't around.

After boosting Will into the buggy, Josiah got in, too. "Would you like to help me hold the reins and guide the *gaul* up the lane?"

Of course, Will was ecstatic and when they came to a halt near the *daadi haus*, he exclaimed, "Wait till I tell my *mamm* I drove a *gaul*—and I'm only five!"

Josiah laughed, just as Anke came down the porch steps. She was watching her feet to be sure she didn't slip on the icy surface, but when she reached the bottom, she glanced up and caught him watching her. Her face broke into a brilliant smile that made Josiah's pulse quicken.

"You've got to scoot into the back now," he told Will. "It's your *ant*'s turn to ride up front with me."

"Denki," Anke said as she settled beside Josiah, tucking the wool blanket he'd handed her around her lap. But after that, she didn't utter a word for the first two miles of their trip. Funny that she couldn't think of anything to say, since she was never at a loss for conversation while Josiah was working on the *daadi haus*. He was

quiet, too—the only one making any noise was Will, who was singing, "Jesus Loves the Little Children" in the back of the carriage.

Still, their silence wasn't unpleasant, just different. *It's so much more relaxing than riding with Keith. That* mann *talked so much it made my head spin,* Anke thought. *And most of the time, he was talking about other people's business.*

Startled to find herself comparing Keith to Josiah, Anke began to sing along with Will. A moment later, Josiah joined in and before she knew it, they'd arrived at his brother's place. Josiah dashed into the barn and returned with the drill, lickety-split. This time when they got back underway, he gave Anke an update on Laura's father, saying he seemed to be doing better and that Victor and Laura were expected home the week after next. After that, conversation flowed easily again until they arrived in town a few minutes later.

They pulled into the lot designated for buggies, which was half a block from the *Englisch* apparel store. As Anke and Will were waiting for Josiah to hitch the horse to the post, a young man and woman buzzed through the field across the street on a snowmobile.

"Did you see that?" Will asked Josiah. "They were going really fast—but I think Star can run even faster. I wish we could race them, don't you?"

"Neh." Josiah sharply chided him, "The *gaul* could get hurt and so could you. And so could the *Englischers* on the snowmobile. That would be *baremlich* for everyone."

"Oh." Will momentarily looked dejected, but Anke knew she couldn't coddle him. It was as important for her to learn to allow others to instruct the child as it was for Will to receive instruction. Yet she was surprised by the severity of Josiah's warning. Will, however, seemed to take it in stride: when she told the boy he had to hold her hand to cross the street, he grasped Josiah's hand, as well. And even after she'd let go of his fingers on the sidewalk, Will and Josiah stayed linked together until they reached the store.

"Are you sure these are Amish boots?" Will asked Anke after she'd selected three pairs from the shelves for him to try on.

"Shoes aren't Amish or *Englisch*, only people are," she warily replied. Sometimes, it seemed there was no end to the amount of explaining she had to do each day in order to help Will understand the difference between the Amish and the *Englisch*. "But *jah*, these are the kind of boots Amish *buwe* wear."

"Is this where Asher and Micah got their

boots?" Will crammed his foot down into the first one Anke gave him to try on.

"*Neh.* They got their boots from someone who outgrew them. The *bu* who gave them their boots moved here from another district. You get to have brand-new boots—that's why these might seem different." Anke was crouched down in front of Will, trying to help him get the second boot on. Why didn't it fit? They were both the same size.

"That hurts," Will complained loudly, drawing the attention of the *Englisch* sales clerk who was hovering near the belt and purse racks, indiscreetly watching them.

"*Ach*—that's because you have two socks on this foot and only one sock on the other." Deciding this pair of boots wasn't a good fit anyway, she told Will to take them off. "Let's see if this pair works instead."

"Did *you* get your boots here?" Will asked Josiah as he pushed his feet into the second pair of boots.

"*Neh.* They don't carry my size. I had to order mine from a catalog."

"I want to order my boots from a catalog, too."

Anke was losing patience. "You're not getting your boots from a catalog—it will take too long for them to arrive. You need new boots now." She noticed an Amish couple milling about in the area, but she didn't recognize them. Maybe they were visitors from the Serenity Ridge district?

"But I want the same kind Josiah has," Will demanded loudly and the Amish woman spun around to glare over her glasses at them.

"Shh. Stop arguing," Anke hissed, pointing a finger at him. "Or you won't get any boots at all."

Will burst into tears. "I don't want any boots. They hurt. They're pinching me."

"Then stand still so I can take them off." Anke tugged the boot, but it wouldn't budge. She tried again, pulling harder. Will's foot abruptly slid free of the boot, but in the process Anke toppled backward and landed on her rump. Physically, she wasn't hurt, but her pride was injured. Especially when the Amish woman clucked her tongue and mumbled something about her not being a good example. Tears sprang to Anke's eyes.

"Here. Let me help you up." Josiah extended his hand and pulled Anke to her feet. For a moment, she was overwhelmed with the desire to nuzzle her face against his chest and weep. Instead, she inched backward, but Josiah still didn't release her hand. "Are you okay?"

She nodded. Will was covering his face with

his arm, hiccupping more than he was crying. Anke wanted to say she thought they should leave now. But she regretted that Josiah had taken them this far out of his way for nothing. "I'm afraid this was a bad idea."

"Do you have anything else you need to buy?" he asked her softly. "You could go browse and I'll help Will try on the last pair of boots. We'll meet you by the cash register."

Anke didn't know if she should accept his offer. "Are you sure?"

Josiah nodded and Anke inched away. Ordinarily, she would have expected an Amish child to behave better than Will was behaving—Amish children learned quite young that tantrums weren't acceptable. But Will *wasn't* an Amish child. As Anke browsed the fabric section of the store, she realized *that* was exactly the problem. Will wasn't being contrary because he wanted his way; he was insisting on wearing the kinds of boots that were exactly like the other boys wore because he wanted to fit in. All along, she'd been emphasizing how important it was that he do what was considered appropriate for Amish children in their district, so of course he'd be upset if he thought he wasn't going to get the "right" kind of boots. She suddenly understood why

Velda said she'd felt like a failure as a mother the other day.

Meandering among the bolts of fabric, Anke was struck by an idea: she'd make Will a pair of pants that were *exactly* like Asher's and Micah's. He could wear them with the sweater she'd been knitting for him.

By the time she reached the cash register, she was smiling again—and so were Will and Josiah, who were waiting for her there. The child was hugging a shoebox. "If at first you don't succeed, try, try again," Josiah whispered to Anke over the boy's head. His breath tickled her ear, making her insides quiver.

"Denki," she whispered back as Will placed the box on the counter. "I'll stand in line— could you two wait for me near the exit? I need to talk to the clerk about something in private."

Josiah took the hint and led the boy away. A few minutes later, she found them sitting side by side on a bench just inside the door. She handed the shoebox to Will, who cradled it in one arm and jumped off the bench to wrap his other arm around her legs.

"Denki for the new boots, *Ant* Anke."

"You're *wilkom.* Do you want to put them on before we go outside?"

He arched his back to look up at her, wide-eyed. "I can wear them *now*?"

"That's why we bought them—to keep your feet warm."

So he sat back down on the bench and removed his sneakers. But before he put on his boots, Anke said, "Wait a second. I have something else for you." She held up a paper bag containing the small gift she'd bought on the sly. But before letting him have it, she said, "There's something in here for Josiah, too. So maybe we should let him open it."

Will nodded eagerly. "This is for me, too?" Josiah repeated in surprise. He reached into the bag Anke gave him and pulled out two pairs of soft dark woolen socks. One pair was child-sized; the other pair was made for an adult.

"Even if you're wearing *gut* boots, it's important to wear warm socks, too," she explained.

"Mine are just like Josiah's," Will noticed, which was why Anke had bought them both a pair. The boy began pulling them on right away.

"*Jah*, except his are bigger." She turned to Josiah and showed him the label. "You said this store didn't carry boots in your size, so I figured you needed extra-long socks. Do you think these will fit all right?"

"They'll fit perfectly. That was very thoughtful. *Denki*, Anke."

She may have given him a pair of wool socks so his feet wouldn't get cold, but the way Josiah said her name made *Anke* feel warm all over.

It was almost one o'clock by the time Josiah, Anke and Will turned into the lane leading to the Bachmans' property.

"I'm sorry that we kept you out so long," she apologized. "But since your work has been interrupted, you might as well have lunch before you get started again, right? I made beef stew last night. It will only take a minute for me to heat it up if you'd like to join us."

I'm in no hurry, Josiah thought. "*Jah,* stew sounds better than the sandwich I brought." He dropped her and Will off in front of the *daadi haus* and then went to stable the horse. As he was walking up the driveway, he noticed Asher and Will running across the lawn to Velda's house.

"Did Will abandon us?" he asked Anke when he came into the kitchen.

"*Jah.* Asher came over and invited him for lunch, so it will just be you and me." Anke gestured for him to take a seat. After she'd served them each a steaming bowl of stew and set a basket of bread in the center of the little table, she said grace. As she buttered a piece of bread, she remarked, "I hope that when Will went inside the main *haus* he remembered to take his boots off. He really loves them. I don't know how you talked him into getting them, but I'm *hallich* you did."

"It wasn't difficult. I just told him that when I was a *bu*, I wore a pair of boots exactly like those." Josiah took a bite of beef; it was incredibly tender. He wondered if that was because Anke was such a good cook or because her brother was a butcher and brought them such great cuts of meat. "I think he was so resistant to the first two pairs because he was scared they weren't 'Amish enough.'" Josiah gave a wry laugh, but Anke set down her spoon, a frown tugging at her mouth.

"*Jah*, I figured that out, too—but not until after he'd had a tantrum. And after *I* did, too." She lowered her eyes. "I'm sorry you had to witness that."

"It's okay. Everyone loses their patience on occasion. But you probably felt a lot more frustrated than how you actually came across." Josiah tipped his head to try to catch her eye, but she still wouldn't look up at him. "For what it's worth, I think you're doing a *wunderbaar* job caring for Will and teaching him about our faith and lifestyle."

"*Denki* for saying that, but…" She shook

her head, as if having an argument with herself. "But sometimes I wonder if I've made a mistake in keeping him with me. I wonder if this has all been too hard on him. Too big of an adjustment. I question whether he would have been better off in foster care. At least that way, he only would have had to adjust to new people, not to an entirely new lifestyle. I think maybe I was being selfish to bring him here."

"Pah!" Josiah snorted, immediately dismissing the notion. "You weren't being selfish, Anke—you were putting your *familye*'s needs first, trying to do what's best for your *schweschder* and nephew. *Jah*, Will might be struggling to adjust to being here, but..." Josiah remembered what Iddo Stoll, the deacon, had said to him the evening they'd eaten supper together. "But he's a lot stronger than you think he is. Besides, you're his *familye* and I doubt any stranger could ever love him the way you do. He's very blessed *Gott* put you in his life."

Even with her head dipped, Josiah could tell the frown was melting from Anke's face. And when she finally looked up, her cheeks were flushed and her eyes were sparkling. "He's very blessed *Gott* put *you* in his life, Josiah— and so am I."

That's how I feel about both of you, too,

Josiah thought. But he didn't dare express it, since the last time he'd felt this way about a woman was when he was courting Jana, and look how that turned out. So instead he replied, "That's very kind of you to say—*denki*." Then he scooped up another spoonful of stew, even though Anke's sentiment had given him such butterflies in his stomach that he hardly felt hungry anymore.

Chapter Ten

"Bye-bye, see you in a while!" Anke waved to Will, Asher, Micah and Millie, who were chasing each other through the snow under Ernest's watchful eye, before she climbed into the buggy with Velda.

It was Saturday afternoon and instead of stabling the horse when he got home from the butcher shop, Ernest had hitched it to the post closer to the house, since Velda and Anke had planned to leave for the grocery store right away. Usually one of the women took turns staying behind with the children, but Ernest said he could manage them on his own, especially since they played together so much better when Will was there with them.

"If it weren't for his jacket, someone passing by would never know Will was *Englisch*," Anke remarked as they pulled down the lane.

On Friday afternoon, she had completed making a pair of "Amish pants," as he called them, for the boy. Once he'd put them on, he hadn't wanted to take them off—he would have slept in them if Anke had let him.

"*Jah*, but does *he* know he's *Englisch*?" Velda asked. "And do *you*?"

Anke twisted sideways to look at her sister-in-law. "What do you mean by that?"

Velda lifted her shoulders in a small shrug. "I wouldn't want him—or you—to forget that just because he dresses and behaves like an Amish *bu* doesn't make him one."

"I'm well aware of that," Anke snapped. "First you were worried he'd be too much of an *Englisch* influence on your *kinner*. But now you're criticizing him because he appears too Amish? You know, sometimes it seems as if there's just no pleasing you." She'd never spoken so bluntly to Velda before, but her sister-in-law had really struck a nerve.

Surprisingly, Velda's response was as gentle as Anke's was harsh. "My intention isn't to be critical. I'm just concerned that one or both of you are losing sight of the fact that he's only going to be here for four more weeks. If he gets the idea he's staying here for *gut*, when Clara returns and takes him back to the *Englisch* world, he'll be crushed. And so will you."

Anke had already had concerns about that herself, but she didn't like to admit them. "We don't know for sure that Clara *will* take him back to the *Englisch* world. We've been praying all this time that she'll repent and return to us and I have faith that will happen."

"I hope it does, but if it doesn't..." Velda wisely didn't complete her sentence. Anke already had gotten her point and she didn't care to talk about it any longer—in part because she knew Velda was right. As fervently as she'd been praying that when Clara completed her recovery program, she'd return home for good, Anke knew that might not happen. The Lord wasn't going to *force* Clara to repent; she had to make that choice for herself. After they'd traveled about a mile, Velda asked, "How much longer until Josiah completes his work on the *daadi haus*?"

"He'll finish sometime this week. Maybe by *Dunnerschdaag.*" Even though Josiah had intended to wrap up the repairs this afternoon, their trip to the shoe store had set his schedule back. Also, he'd mentioned a few other things he'd noticed needed fixing. For instance, he still wanted to add another step to the porch staircase so it wouldn't be so difficult for Will to get up it. So Josiah estimated he'd be finished with all the extra repairs by Thursday.

"Dunnerschdaag?" Velda giggled. "At this rate, Will's going to be long gone by the time Josiah finishes the repairs."

Now Anke was doubly irritated; first, because of Velda mentioning Will leaving again and second because it sounded as if she was criticizing Josiah. "He does excellent work and he's actually very efficient. But the *daadi haus* was in worse shape than we thought it was. There's a lot to do."

Velda threw back her head and laughed. "You don't really believe that, do you, Anke? He's stalling on purpose so he can spend more time around you."

Do you really think so? Anke wanted to ask, suddenly feeling as giddy as a schoolgirl. Just because it was impractical for her to court anyone didn't mean she wasn't flattered about the possibility of Josiah being drawn to her.

"Oh, look at you blush! You want him to be your suitor, don't you?" Her sister-in-law teased. "Maybe I should *kumme* over with the *kinner* during the day and chaperone the two of you?"

"There wouldn't be room for you to *kumme* over with the *kinner*. We'd have to squeeze together like sardines in a can," Anke told her.

Velda grew serious. "*Jah*, I know the place is really tiny...and I feel bad you've been cramped up in there, but I hope you understand why I still think it's prudent to keep a little space between the *kinner* and Will."

"*Jah*. I do," Anke assured her. "And don't worry about us. We're not cramped—we're cozy." And by that, she didn't just mean her and Will; she meant Josiah, too.

From Anke's remark yesterday, it's safe to assume she's as fond of me as I am of her, Josiah thought as he moved a handheld manual sander across the floorboards in the bedroom. *Just because I had a* baremlich *experience courting Jana doesn't mean the same thing is going to happen here.* Moving to Maine was supposed to be a fresh start for him, so why shouldn't that include a new romantic relationship, as well as a new district and a new job?

These were the same thoughts he'd been thinking all morning. Actually, they had kept him tossing and turning throughout the night, too. Now his mind was made up: he was going to ask Anke if he could be her suitor. The question now was, *when* could he ask her? Will was always around. *I know—I could ask if she wants to go snowshoeing with me tomorrow after* kurrich *and talk to her about it then! I'm sure Velda and Ernest would take Will home with them.*

Having figured out his strategy, Josiah was so eager to put his plan into action that he stopped sanding and went outside to see if he could spy Anke and Velda returning from the grocery store in the buggy. Instead, he spotted the children and Ernest gathered beneath a barren maple tree halfway across the yard. Ernest was holding Charity in one arm and using his other arm to push Millie on the swing. It seemed like a strange winter activity, but the children apparently were enjoying it because they'd formed a line to take a turn.

Josiah was crossing the yard to ask if Ernest needed a hand, when the buggy rolled up the driveway. So he switched course and went to help Anke carry the groceries inside, instead. *Now is my chance*, he thought, hoping Will would stay outdoors a little longer.

They'd made it to the porch when the little boy called out, "*Ant* Anke, look at me! Am I going as high as my *mamm*?" He was pumping his legs and sweeping back and forth in an arc through the air without any help from Ernest.

"You're going even higher!" Anke answered.

Josiah followed her into the house and set the two bags of groceries on the table. She thanked him and immediately began putting the food away, buzzing around the kitchen as quickly as a hummingbird. It made him so nervous he almost retreated into the bedroom to resume sanding the floor again. But he knew Will could return at any minute and he didn't want to waste this opportunity. So, without even waiting to get Anke's attention, Josiah hastily blurted out, "Would you like to go snowshoeing with me after *kurrich* tomorrow?"

She turned from the cupboard to face him, a surprised look in her eyes. "I would, but..." she said slowly, indicating she was about to give a reason why she couldn't. Josiah braced himself for disappointment. "But I don't have any snowshoes. Whenever I've gone snowshoeing, I've borrowed a pair from Faith's *schweschder.*"

Relieved, Josiah offered, "You could use Laura's—I'm sure she won't mind. I'll bring them with me to *kurrich.*"

"In that case, I'd love to go, provided Velda and Ernest don't object to taking Will home with them."

Why should they—you've been taking care of their kinner *for years*, Josiah thought. But for what felt like the hundredth time, he reminded himself that that was none of his business. Besides, even if Anke couldn't go snowshoeing this Sunday, the important thing was that she'd said yes in the first place. Emboldened, Josiah inwardly resolved, *If tomorrow doesn't work out, then I'll just keep asking her until we finally get time together by ourselves.*

After supper, Anke rocked in front of the woodstove as she continued knitting the sweater she'd begun for Will. The boy, meanwhile, bent over the pad of paper on his lap, drawing something he said he didn't want Anke to see yet. He was so intent on sketching that for once, he didn't ask her any questions, which allowed Anke's mind to wander.

For someone who'd claimed she didn't need romance in her life, she was exceptionally happy that Josiah had asked her to go snowshoeing with him tomorrow. In New Hope, there were only two reasons why a single Amish man spent an afternoon alone with a single Amish woman. The first was that he was about to ask to be her suitor and the second was that they were already courting. Of course, Anke wasn't sure what the customs were in Illinois, so she didn't want to make any assumptions. But just the fact that Josiah wanted to spend his day off with her made Anke believe he liked her in a special way—which was how *she* felt about him, too.

Still, enjoying someone's company wasn't

the same as courting and if Josiah did ask her to walk out, Anke was no longer sure how she'd answer. Up until Thursday, if he had proposed courtship, she would have turned him down. She would have said she didn't have time for a suitor—she had her family's needs to focus on. She would have explained that the men who'd courted her in the past wound up resenting the way she'd put her family's needs above her courtship with them. Anke might have told Josiah she valued his friendship too much to risk falling out with him.

However, on Thursday after they'd come home from town, Josiah had made it very clear that he understood Anke's commitment to doing what she thought was best for her family. He even seemed to appreciate that quality in her. And he'd been a huge help with Will, especially in the apparel store, when the child had thrown a tantrum. Anke couldn't imagine anyone else she'd courted ever being that patient with the child—or with *her.*

Maybe it's possible to serve my family and *have a suitor after all,* she mused. *Maybe I just needed to find the right* mann.

Realizing she'd dropped a stitch, Anke set her knitting on her lap and reminded herself that Josiah *hadn't* asked to court her. Furthermore, she hadn't even asked Velda yet if she and Ernest could take care of Will after church. So Anke didn't need to decide right this minute what she'd say if Josiah happened to bring up the topic of courtship tomorrow. She'd have to pray about it later, so she'd be better prepared to respond if necessary.

"It's time for you to go to bed, Will," she told her nephew. "We have to get up early for *kurrich* tomorrow. Do you want to show me what you've drawn?"

Will slid off his chair and brought the paper to her. "It's you and me and Josiah. See? That's his hat."

"I see. And we're all holding hands, aren't we?" Anke surmised the picture was inspired by their trip into town on Thursday.

"*Jah. Mamm* and my *daed* used to hold hands with me, too. *Mamm* said they'd swing me really high."

Anke was troubled that Will seemed to be associating Josiah and her with Clara and her boyfriend. Did that mean he felt like Anke and Josiah were replacing his parents? Maybe her sister-in-law was right. Maybe he was beginning to think that he was staying here permanently. "It's a very nice picture," she said. "Now let's go wash your face and brush your teeth."

After Will had gotten into his pajamas and

Anke had prayed with him, the boy crawled into bed. "Didn't you forget something?" she asked him. When he stared blankly at her, she prompted, "The screw jars." Although he'd looked at the photo from his book bag, he hadn't transferred a screw from the clear jar to the blue jar the way he did every night to mark how many days were left until he saw his mother.

"Do we have to do that?"

"*Neh*, I guess not." *Maybe he's adjusting better now*, Anke thought hopefully. But she decided she'd better not assume. "Why don't you want to?"

"Pretty soon there won't be any screws in the white jar. That means I have to go back to the 'partment."

Anke inhaled sharply, realizing that by not transferring a screw, Will thought he could somehow keep his visit from ending. As earnestly as she was praying that he could stay there permanently, too, she realized it might not happen. Clara might complete her recovery and return to the *Englisch* world. Velda was right—if Anke didn't keep that possibility in the forefront of Will's mind, when it happened, he'd be devastated. So she said, "*Jah*. But it also means you get to see your *mamm*. And she can't wait to see you."

Will blinked a few times, thinking. Then he got up and went over to where the jars were balanced on the low end table Velda had given them to use. He reached into the clear jar, took out a screw and deposited it into the blue jar. *Tink.*

One more day gone, Anke thought. After she'd tucked Will in, she sat on the edge of his bed for a long time, watching him sleep and thinking about how attached he'd already grown to his family here. It was what Anke had wanted: for them to be close and to come to love each other. She hadn't really considered how brutal it would be for them to separate if Clara didn't return to the Amish.

What am I supposed to do? Her question was part prayer, part lament. It wasn't as if Anke or his cousins could pull back from the child; that would be cruel. They were his family. *But maybe I could at least put a little distance between him and Josiah, so he doesn't grow even more attached.* Anke realized that meant for now—with the exception of when the three of them went out for pizza together— she was also going to have to put more distance between Josiah and herself, so that Will wouldn't see them as parental figures.

I suppose that resolves the issue of what my answer will be if Josiah asks to court me, she thought sadly. But why put either of them in that position? It seemed kinder to cancel their snowshoeing expedition altogether, yet she didn't know what reason to give him. She didn't want to say she was afraid that Will was beginning to see them as his substitute parents, or even as a couple—that would have sounded too forward, especially if he wasn't considering asking to court her. *I guess I could tell him I didn't want to be away from Will for that long after all*, she decided. And it was true; the more she thought about her nephew going back to the *Englisch* world in four weeks or so, the less willing Anke was to miss even an afternoon with him now.

On Sunday morning, Josiah remembered what Omer and Keith had said about scrambling to take the front row at church so their children wouldn't have to be distracted by looking at an *Englisch* boy. He was concerned Anke's and Will's feelings would be hurt if they recognized other people were avoiding them. So he decided he would sit beside them during the service. But when he entered the church's large gathering room, he realized that not everyone seemed to feel the same way Omer and Keith felt; with the exception of an elderly couple, no one else had joined them in the front row.

However, since Josiah didn't have any relatives to sit with, he figured it wouldn't be inappropriate for him to join the Bachman family anyway. Anke was sitting at the end of the bench; Will sat on her left. Asher was beside him, then Velda, who was holding Charity. On the other side of Velda were Millie, Micah and Ernest. There was just enough space to Anke's right for Josiah to slide onto the bench beside her. Looking straight ahead, she gave a slight nod to acknowledge his presence, but didn't say hello because it would have been considered rude to chat with each other after they'd entered the gathering room.

Josiah said a silent prayer, asking God to keep Will from feeling overwhelmed. Amish mothers usually brought handkerchiefs to tie into various shapes to keep their little ones quiet during the service, which lasted for three hours. They also brought pretzels or crackers and raisins for the children to snack on. Still, three hours was a long time for a child to sit still, especially for an *Englisch* boy who wasn't even school age yet and who had never been to an Amish church.

When everyone rose to sing the opening hymn, Will stood on cue, copying his cousin

Asher. The second song sung in every Amish service was always "The *Loblied*." It sounded more like a chant and in New Hope the Amish sang the traditional German version. During the opening verse, Josiah heard Will's voice, soft but distinct. *I hope he's not going to ask Anke a lot of questions,* he worried. *Otherwise, there are bound to be complaints and criticisms about her bringing her nephew to church.*

Anke leaned toward the child and then stood up straight again. Even as the other men's and women's voices filled the room, Josiah could still hear the child's voice in the background. *Isn't Anke going to quiet him?* Josiah wondered. But then he realized the boy wasn't talking; he was singing, too. He strained to hear him incant the words perfectly in German, although he couldn't have known what they meant. Will stopped singing after the third verse, but Josiah was astounded that Anke had taught him to memorize as much of the song as she had.

In the corner of his eye he saw her hand move up to her cheek time and time again— she was blotting tears from her skin. That was when it struck him that she hadn't taught him the song at all. Josiah would have heard them practicing. He figured out that Anke was crying because it was Clara who must have taught

Will to sing like that, and Josiah got a little choked up, too.

For the rest of the service Will was very quiet. But toward the very end, he whispered loudly enough in Anke's ear for Josiah to hear him say, "I have to go to the bathroom." As soon as the closing hymn was sung, Josiah stepped aside to allow Anke and the boy to scramble out of the room. He would have liked to at least say hello to her before lunch preparations got underway, but knowing they were going snowshoeing later curbed his disappointment. *If a little Englisch bu has the patience to remain quiet through a three-hour church service, I suppose I can wait another hour to ask Anke if I can be her suitor,* he decided.

Lovina Bawell, Honor's mother, came up to Will as he stood with Anke in line to use the bathroom. "I heard you singing," she remarked. "Did your *ant* Anke teach you that song?"

"*Neh.* My *mamm* sings it at nighttime when her nerves feel bad," Will answered openly. "It makes her sleepy."

Anke cringed to herself, wondering how Lovina would react to the child's frank admission about Clara. But the older woman just nodded and said, "It's *gut* to sing hymns or to pray when we're upset." Then she smiled and walked away.

Clara must have been upset frequently for him to learn the first three stanzas, she thought. Yet she also felt a little surge of hope; at least her sister had taken *something* about her Amish faith and background to heart.

After Will had used the bathroom, she sent him off to play with the other children under the care of three teenage girls whose turn it was to keep them occupied while the older women prepared lunch. Anke felt so dismayed that she was going to have to cancel her snow-shoeing outing with Josiah that she could hardly concentrate on what the other women were chatting about. But when it was her turn to eat and she sat down beside Velda, her sis-ter-in-law whispered, "Have you heard what everyone's saying about Will?"

"Neh," she replied, bristling. *And I don't think I want to.*

"They were amazed that an *Englisch bu* knows 'The *Loblied.*' Someone even said you'd put them to shame by teaching him that song before they've taught their *kinner.*"

"I didn't teach him—Clara did."

"Jah, that's what Lovina told us," Velda said, sitting up straighter. "You should have seen the looks on the other *weibsleit's* faces!"

Anke had to smile to herself; just two weeks ago Velda was ashamed of being associated with Clara. Now she was bordering on being prideful about her *Englisch* sister-in-law. Changing the subject, Anke told her that she had to speak with Josiah briefly and asked if Velda could take Will to the buggy with the other children.

After Velda agreed, the two women finished their meals quickly so they could return to the kitchen to help with the last of the dishes. Then Anke dashed outside to the hitching rail. She saw Josiah's horse, but she couldn't find him. She hurried back toward the church to look for him inside again, but before she rounded the corner of the building, Keith Harnish stopped her.

"Whoa. Where are you going so fast?" he asked.

"Hello, Keith. Have you seen Josiah?"

"He may have taken off so he could go hang out with some *Englisch* alcoholics like your *schweschder*."

Anke crossed her arms against her chest. "First of all, if you're going to refer to my *schweschder*, please call her by her name. It's Clara. Secondly, I don't know what you mean by your remark, but I don't think you're at all funny."

"I'm not trying to be—I'm completely serious. Last year, Josiah was caught red-handed supplying beer to *Englisch* teenagers in Illinois. It was in the back of his buggy. Somebody captured the entire incident on their cell phone and posted it on social media. It went viral, which is the *Englisch* way of saying it spread like wildfire. I've watched the clip myself."

"Now I know you're joking. You've always claimed that you never use your cell phone to look at *Englisch* social media," Anke challenged him. "You only use it for business purposes."

"I didn't watch the clip on *my* phone. A customer showed it to me. He came into the hardware store the same day Josiah did and he recognized him from social media right away because of his flaming mop of hair."

"I'm sure he's not the only Amish man with red hair in Illinois." Anke rubbed her forehead. The combination of the frigid breeze and Keith's nonsense was giving her a headache. "I've gotten to know Josiah well enough that I'm certain that when he makes a commitment, he sticks to it. That includes his commitment to abide by the *Ordnung*. He'd never do what you're describing."

"He's only been here two weeks, so what

makes you think you know what he's really like?" Keith challenged. "I'm telling you, Anke, you should stay away from Josiah. People are known by the company they keep. And you've already got a strike against you because of your alcoholic *schweschder.*"

She balled her gloved fingers into a fist to keep herself from shouting, *My* schweschder's *name is Clara and I don't care what you saw on social media, I know what kind of* mann *Josiah is!* Anke's head was really throbbing now, so she took a deep breath and let it out. She was about to say that she'd be glad to be known by the company she kept because she considered Josiah to be compassionate, industrious and funny, but just then, someone cleared his throat behind her.

Although he'd only caught a snippet of their conversation, it was clear to Josiah that Keith had been warning Anke to stay away from him. *But why would he say that unless...unless he somehow found out what happened in Illinois?* Josiah realized that must have been it: why else would Keith have said that people were known by the company they kept? Feeling both mortified and infuriated, he could barely keep his voice from shaking as he greeted them. "Hi, Anke. Hi, Keith."

Anke said hello, but Keith muttered, "See you." Then he walked way.

Figuring he could talk to Anke about what Keith had told her once they were in the buggy, Josiah asked, "Are you all set to go snowshoeing?"

"I—I'm afraid I can't g-go with you today after all," she stuttered nervously.

"Really? Velda and Ernest wouldn't agree to watch Will for you?"

"*Neh*, that's not the problem. It's that…it's that Will's only here for a few weeks and I want to spend as much time with him as I can."

Josiah wasn't buying her excuse. It seemed to him that she'd changed her mind because of what Keith had told her. She wouldn't do that, would she? He bluntly replied, "I don't understand why that didn't occur to you yesterday. Did something else happen to change your mind?"

She rubbed her brow and closed her eyes and then opened them again before answering. "*Jah*. I'm getting a *koppweh*, so I'm sorry I'm not really up for discussing it right now. But what it *kummes* down to is that, well, I don't know how to say this exactly…"

With a sinking feeling in his gut, Josiah said it for her. "You don't think we should socialize together."

"*Jah*. But only because of Will. He's so young and impressionable and I wouldn't want him to get the idea that, you know, that we're a couple—"

Josiah had heard enough. Cutting Anke off, he snidely retorted, "I wouldn't want him to get that idea either, because we're *not*. So it's fine by me if we keep our distance from each other." He turned on his heel to leave, but she caught him by his arm.

Anke's eyelashes were beaded with tears. "I'm sorry if my decision upsets you, Josiah. But I thought you'd understand that I have to do what's best for my nephew and—"

"I understand all right. And as soon as I finish the repairs on the *daadi haus*, I'll be out of your hair. But *you're* going to have to be the one to tell Will we're not going out for pizza together, because when *I* agree to do something, I don't break my word." Josiah yanked his arm from her grasp and strode across the lawn to his buggy, both hurt and seething.

He unhitched his horse from the rail and as he started toward home, Josiah brooded, *This situation with Anke reminds me almost exactly of what happened with Jana—but at least Jana gave me the benefit of the doubt, even if she did assume it was a member of my family who had been drinking.* Anke hadn't even heard his side of the story before she decided she no longer wanted to associate with him. And for her to use Will as an excuse was like rubbing salt in Josiah's wounds. All he'd ever done was try to have a good influence on the child!

It was maddening to him that he'd risked his own reputation by helping Anke host her alcoholic sister's son, yet she had the nerve to distance herself from *him*, when Josiah had never even had so much as a drop of fermented cider. He felt every bit as betrayed as he did after he'd tried to help Jana's brother. He also felt incredibly foolish to have made the same mistake twice. *I just don't learn, do I?* he chastised himself. *How could I have thought Anke was someone I'd want to court? Anyone who behaves like that isn't even a friend!*

But she was his employer—for a couple more days, at least. *Tomorrow I can put the finishing touches on the bedroom floor and I should be able to wrap up the rest of the repairs by* Dinnschdaag *afternoon*, he thought. Yes, he'd claimed it would probably take him until Thursday to complete a few extra projects he'd agreed to do—but that was because he was drawing them out so he could spend more time with Anke and her nephew. Now he couldn't finish them fast enough.

* * *

Once they arrived home and got out of the buggy, Ernest stayed in the barn to unhitch the horse. The four older children ran toward the house, while the two women strolled up the driveway behind them. "Are you okay?" Velda asked, shifting Charity in her arms. "You seem upset about something."

Anke had managed to contain her tears all the way home. But she was afraid that the floodgates would open up if she told her sister-in-law why she really felt so crushed, so she said, "I have a *koppweh*, that's all."

"Then you should go take a nap. Will can play with our *kinner*. Ernest told them they can all take two turns on the swing, then they'll *kumme* inside to color some pictures, have a snack and take a nap. Asher will be thrilled to let Will use his bed so he'll have an excuse to sleep on a cot like Will gets to do in the *daadi haus*."

After claiming she intended to spend as much time as she could with her nephew before she left, Anke felt too guilty to accept Velda's offer. "*Neh*. That's okay. It'll probably go away once I warm up and have a cup of tea."

"Then you should just go have a cup of tea by yourself and enjoy a little peace and quiet," Velda suggested. "You've always helped Ernest and me with our *kinner*. I don't think I've ever appreciated it as much as I have these past two weeks, when you haven't been in the *haus* to give me a hand. So why not allow me to return the favor? Or is it that you don't want Will to play in such a messy *haus*? Because I promise you, I've been keeping up with my housework a lot better these past couple of days and I won't serve him soup from a can, either."

Anke gave a wan smile. "I'm not at all worried about those things. I suppose a nap might be a *gut* idea, if you're sure you don't mind?"

"Not at all. Sleep as long as you like."

So Anke returned to the *daadi haus* alone. But by the time she'd stoked the fire in the woodstove and made a cup of tea, she was weeping too hard to drink it. *I thought Josiah was different*, she cried to herself as she pushed the rocker back and forth with her feet. *I really believed he respected that I have to put Will's needs above my own.*

She could have accepted it if Josiah expressed disappointment because she'd changed her mind about going snowshoeing. After all, she'd really been looking forward to spending time with him alone, too. But he'd acted even sulkier than Keith or her other suitors had acted, not even allowing her to finish her sentences. *Keith was right—I don't know him as well as I thought I did.* Not that she believed there was an iota of merit to what Keith had said about Josiah supplying alcohol to *Englisch* teenagers. But Anke never would have expected him to react to her decision the way he did.

And she certainly never expected him to cancel their plans to go out for pizza when he completed the *daadi haus* repairs. It was completely unreasonable for him to pin the blame on her because she'd been the one to say she didn't think they should socialize. *I didn't mean we couldn't still go out for pizza. Or even that we should never socialize again,* she thought. Josiah would have known that if he had allowed her to finish talking instead of being so defensive. *How am I ever going to tell Will we're not going out to his favorite kind of restaurant?* she cried to herself. *He's going to be crushed.*

Once again, Anke remembered what her mother had said about how a man could win a woman's heart by how he treated her child. *A* mann *can break a* weibsmensch's *heart by the way he treats her child, too,* she thought. And that was exactly what Josiah had done to her.

Chapter Eleven

The good thing about Will sleeping in the same room with Anke was that she was so concerned he'd hear her weeping that she couldn't give in to her tears on Sunday night. However, she'd cried so much on Sunday afternoon that she still woke with puffy eyes and a pink nose on Monday morning.

After dressing and brushing her hair, she returned to the living room to wake her nephew. "Will," she said, touching his shoulder. "It's time to get up. We're taking your *onkel* to work, remember?"

Yesterday afternoon, Anke had grown so distraught about the idea of being around Josiah all day when he came to work on the *daadi haus*, she asked Ernest if she could use the buggy. She decided she could stop in at Millers' Restaurant to collect her money for any aprons that had sold the previous week. Later in the afternoon, she intended to take all the children to the library, while Velda stayed home with Charity. But first, she and Will had to bring Ernest to the butcher shop.

"Will," she repeated. "Wake up."

As the boy drowsily rose and got dressed, Anke went into the kitchen to scramble eggs. "Aren't we going to wait to see if Josiah wants to eat with us, too?" he asked when he came into the kitchen.

"*Neh.* By the time we return, he'll be hard at work. If we keep distracting him every morning the way we've been doing, he won't be able to finish our rooms. We don't want that to happen, do we?"

Will shrugged. "I like sleeping in the living room."

"I think you'll like sleeping in your own bedroom just as well, now that Josiah has fixed it up." Anke had to admit that he had done beautiful work; the floors looked nicer and smoother than those in the main house and she could no longer feel a draft coming from any of the windows. "You'll be as snug as a bug."

"How many more days until Josiah's finished?"

"I—I'm not sure," she hedged. "A couple, maybe."

"*Gut.* Then we get to go out for pizza!" Will exclaimed. Anke still didn't know how she was going to break it to him that they weren't going out for supper together. Will must have noticed her frowning because he asked, "What's wrong, *Ant* Anke?"

"Nothing, but no more talk about pizza. You haven't even eaten your breakfast yet," she said, rising from the table to get a piece of paper and a pen.

"What's that?" Will asked when he saw her affix the note she'd written on the outside of the door with a tack some twenty minutes later as they were leaving.

"It's a message for Josiah, so he knows we're not going to be here today."

"Not at all?"

Not if I can help it, Anke thought. "Well, this morning we have errands and then *Ant* Velda invited us to eat lunch at the other *haus.* And after that, we're going to the library. So we won't be coming back until later this afternoon and then we'll have to pick up your *onkel* again. Why do you ask?"

"Because I have to give Josiah the picture I made for him," Will said and hopped down the porch steps.

Anke had forgotten all about the picture, so on the way to the barn she silently prayed,

Please, Lord, don't let Josiah's anger at me affect the way he responds to Will. Then she reluctantly added, *And please help me not to feel so angry at Josiah, either.*

When Josiah reached the *daadi haus*, he pulled a note with his name on it off the front door. The note read, "Will and I will be gone for most of the day until around two or three o'clock. If he says anything about going to the pizzeria, please don't let on that we aren't going—I haven't told him yet."

Don't worry—I won't, Josiah thought. As he'd said yesterday, it was Anke's responsibility, not his, to break the news to Will that she didn't want them to socialize anymore. *Apparently, she doesn't want to be in the same haus with me, either*, Josiah concluded, because she'd never been away for so long during the day. He might have found her avoidance to be insulting, except he didn't want to be in her company, either.

Without Anke and Will there to invite him to join them for a snack or lunch break, Josiah got a lot more done than usual. So at two forty-five when he accidentally cracked the final length of floor molding he was installing, he decided he'd call it a day. *I need to purchase more molding and by the time I go into town and return, it will be after four o'clock anyway,* he rationalized. More important, he wanted to leave before Anke and Will returned.

On the back of the note Anke had written to him, Josiah scribbled, "Went to the hardware store. Be back tomorrow." Rather than posting it to the door, he decided to leave it on the coffee table in the living room. When he set it down, he noticed one of Will's drawings. Although the picture was rudimentary, it was still far better than any Josiah had ever seen a child make. He could easily tell that it was an illustration of three people: a man and a woman holding hands with the boy in between them.

That's Anke, Will and me, he thought, recognizing himself because the boy had depicted him wearing a hat. Immediately, he was overwhelmed with regret. *I've always done my best to keep my word. Now I'm going to break a promise to a* kind? Just because Anke was the one who had decided they shouldn't socialize any more didn't alleviate Josiah's guilt. *Will is going to feel as let down by me as I felt by her.* It wasn't an experience he'd wish on anyone, especially not a child.

Is she really so fearful of associating with me that she'd rather allow Will to get hurt than to go out together for one meal? It seemed a hypocritical thing to do, considering how much it had hurt her when other people behaved that way toward her and Will, but Josiah figured there wasn't anything he could do to change her mind. He set the drawing back on the table and headed out to the barn to hitch his buggy.

His intention was to go to the *Englisch* hardware store because even though the prices were higher there, he wouldn't have to listen to Keith make wisecracks about his past. But halfway into town, he thought, *I'm sure Keith has already spread the word about the golf course video, so I might as well get used to whatever he or anyone else says about me.* Josiah was tired of trying to hide his past, as if he'd done something shameful. *Maybe it's better if people know sooner rather than later, because that's how I'll find out who might be my friends and who might be...like Keith. Or Anke.*

So ten minutes later, he strode into the hardware store, his head held high. "Hi, Omer. Hi, Keith," he loudly greeted the two men. They were standing near the front counter, huddled over a cell phone. "What's new?"

Keith hid the phone from view and began fiddling with the receipt tape on the cash register. But Omer blatantly confessed, "Keith just showed me a video of a red-headed man who was caught with beer in the back of his buggy. He's tried to tell me it was you, but he's pulling my leg, isn't he?"

Josiah shook his head. "*Neh.* That was me all right. But it wasn't my beer. I've never touched any alcoholic drink in my life. Although I can't prove it, I suspect those *Englisch* teenagers you also saw in the video stashed their beer in my buggy so they wouldn't get in trouble."

Keith ridiculed, "Do you really expect anyone to believe that?"

"*Gott* knows that it's the truth and His opinion of Josiah is the one that matters most," a man's voice said loudly as he emerged from a side aisle. It was Iddo Stoll, the deacon, and he was glaring at Keith and Omer. "Whether you choose to believe it or not is your business. But when I hear you spreading falsehoods in our community, then it becomes *my* business, too. So you *menner* can expect a home visit to discuss what *Gott*'s Word has to say about slandering your neighbor." He stepped past the cash register and doddered out the door, leaving all three men slack jawed and speechless.

A few minutes after Josiah had purchased the molding he needed and he was on his way home, he reflected on what had transpired in the hardware store. He was very grateful that Iddo had come to his defense, and he expected today would be the last time Keith or Omer would have anything disparaging to say to him about the incident in Illinois. He also appreciated that the deacon had pointed out what Josiah should have concluded a long time ago: God's opinion of him was the one that mattered most.

But that didn't mean he wasn't affected by people's opinions of him, too. Especially when one of those people was someone he'd grown to like very much. Someone he'd dreamed of courting. Someone who had seemed so trustworthy that even now, he couldn't believe he'd been as wrong about her as she was about him.

On Tuesday morning, Anke was so distraught about anticipating telling Will that they wouldn't be going out for pizza with Josiah that she got sick to her stomach. And while she was in the bathroom, the boy happily answered the front door when the carpenter arrived.

"*Gudermariye*, Josiah." Will's enthusiastic greeting was loud enough for Anke to hear down the hall. Then he announced, "*Ant* Anke has a *bauchweh*. She's in the bathroom getting sick." Anke quickly rinsed her mouth and opened the door.

"Oh. Are you sick, too?" Josiah sounded concerned.

"*Neh.* Look, I made this for you."

In the quiet pause that followed, Anke stood in the hallway, holding her breath and praying that Josiah wouldn't be as ungracious about receiving the picture as he'd been about accepting the cookies Will had made for him the previous week.

"I like this drawing. You put a lot of detail into it. I notice the *mann* and *bu* are wearing the same-colored socks," Josiah finally said, and Ankle exhaled in relief.

"That's because it's me and you. And this is *Ant* Anke. See her eyes? That color is called turtle blue."

Anke pressed her hand over her mouth, suppressing a giggle.

"You mean turquoise blue?" Josiah asked.

"*Jah.* Isn't it pretty?"

Anke stepped into the room before Josiah could answer. "*Gudermariye,*" she said coolly to Josiah. "Will, *kumme* into the kitchen to have your breakfast. Let Josiah get to work."

"Do you want to eat with us?" Will invited him.

Anke quickly spoke up. "I'm not making breakfast this morning because I have a *bauch-*

weh, remember? I doubt Josiah wants to eat cold cereal."

"*Neh*, I don't," he confirmed just as quickly. "I'm going to get right to work. I'll be finished with Will's bedroom today. I can move his bed in there when I'm done if you want me to."

Anke was surprised that Josiah was being so accommodating. *It must be because I prayed he wouldn't take his anger at me out on Will.* Then she remembered she'd also prayed that *she* wouldn't feel so angry at Josiah, either, and she said, "*Denki.* I'd appreciate that."

"I can help you move it," Will volunteered.

"You probably won't be here—we're going to Sovilla's *haus* today with your *gschwis-chderkinner.*" After church on Sunday, Arleta had invited a group of mothers with young children to go to her house on Tuesday after lunch. The adults were going to work on sewing projects while the children played outside.

Their neighbor down the road, Martha Ropp, was going to pick them up and take them home, since she and her three children had been invited, too. Anke knew it would be a tight squeeze in the buggy, but she didn't care. Nor did she mind that she'd had an upset stomach. The only thing that mattered was spending as much time away from the *daadi haus* as she could until Josiah was done with the repairs and left for good.

It was nearly four o'clock and Josiah had completed everything he'd agreed to repair inside the *daadi haus* and he'd moved Will's bed into the bedroom, too. If he hurried, he could add an extra step to the porch stairs and leave before Anke and Will returned. Although he still had misgivings about not following through with his commitment to take Will out for pizza, Josiah knew he didn't have any other choice in the matter. But he didn't want to be around when the child realized it was his last day there.

As he was prying the board off the bottom step so he could reconfigure it, he heard a vehicle drive up the lane. *Someone must have turned down into the driveway by mistake*, he thought. *I hope they're not lost, because I don't want to take the time to give them directions.*

Unfortunately, when he glanced over his shoulder, he noticed an *Englisch* woman with purplish hair get out of the back seat. "Nobody's home," he shouted to her as she began walking toward the main house. "Can I help you with something?"

The woman turned to face him. "I'm looking for Anke Bachman," she called back.

Josiah took a few steps closer so he wouldn't have to keep yelling to be heard. As he approached, he thought, *She looks familiar. Have I seen her in town before?* Just as he reached the driveway, he realized why he seemed to recognize her. *She looks just like Will—that's his mother! That's Clara!* Josiah came to a dead halt.

"Anke's not here," he said. "No one is. They should be back within an hour."

"An hour?" she repeated, biting her thumbnail. "Okay, well, I'll just have to wait, then."

Josiah was so stupefied he couldn't seem to move as he watched her return to the car. She opened the door and got in, but the driver didn't reverse direction. *Are they just going to idle there until Anke returns?* Josiah wondered. He couldn't imagine Velda's reaction to finding an *Englisch* car in the driveway, much less, to seeing Clara with purple hair. But a moment later, Anke's sister got out of the vehicle again. "That's the last time I ever use your service!" she shouted, slamming the door. The car sped away as Clara hurried across the lawn to the main house again.

Josiah shook his head and resumed his work on the porch step, but his mind could hardly concentrate on what his hands were doing. *Why is Clara here? She couldn't have com-*

pleted the recovery program already—she's only been there a little over two weeks. His stomach felt knotted up with dread. *What is Anke going to do when she sees her? And how is Will going to feel?*

"It's locked," Clara announced, jarring him from his thoughts. Josiah hadn't realized she'd crept up right beside him.

"What?" He stopped what he was doing and stood up to speak to her.

"The door to the main house is locked. We never locked the door when I lived here," she explained, biting her pinkie nail this time. Didn't she have any gloves? It was freezing out here. "I'm Clara, Anke's sister. She's been taking care of my son, Will."

"*Jah.* I know," Josiah replied flatly. He begrudgingly told her his name, too.

"It figures. Everyone knows everything about everybody here. You probably know *why* she's been taking care of him, too, don't you?" After Josiah nodded, Clara momentarily glanced down at her feet. Then she looked up and changed the subject. "So, did you buy this place from my family or are you just renting it?"

"Neither. Anke hired me to make repairs so it's livable for her and Will."

Clara's eyes went big and round, just as

her son's always did when he was astonished. "They've been staying out here?" After Josiah nodded, she mumbled dolefully, "I should have known Velda wouldn't allow them in the main house with her."

Regardless of how he felt about her sister, Josiah didn't want Clara to worry about her son's living conditions. "It's actually pretty cozy inside," he consoled her.

She immediately perked up. "Good. Then I'll wait in there where it's warm." Bypassing the bottom step, she bounded up the stairs and into the *daadi haus* before Josiah could object.

It's not my haus *anyway, so I can't stop her*, he thought. Besides, now that Clara was there, he had an even more urgent reason to finish his work and leave before Anke and Will returned, so he got back to it. Even though his mind was swirling with concerns about why the boy's mother had returned, Josiah managed to stay focused and he finished installing the step within fifteen minutes. *Now all I need to do is collect my tools from the bedroom and I can get out of here.*

When he pushed open the door, he discovered Clara holding a handful of Will's socks over an open duffel bag. Maybe it was because he noticed she had dropped the pair that Anke had given to the boy—the socks he loved so much because they matched Josiah's—on the floor, but he couldn't stop himself from blurting out, "What do you think you're doing with those?"

"I'm packing. That's why I'm here—I came to get Will. I want to have his things ready so we can leave as soon as he returns." She deposited his clothes into the bag and added defiantly, "Not that it's any of *your* business—or anyone else's. Will is *my* child."

Josiah had been telling himself the same thing for two weeks; he wasn't a member of the Bachman family, so what they did wasn't any of his business. But he no longer cared whether he had any right to voice his opinion or not. For Will's sake, he was going to speak his mind. "*Jah*, Will *is* your *kind*. But if you take him away from here before you've completed your recovery program, you'll risk losing him for *gut*. Is that what you want?"

Clara turned her back to Josiah and zipped the duffel bag, wordlessly indicating she was going to carry through with her intention to take the boy away from New Hope. Away from Anke.

Softening his tone, Josiah pleaded, "Please don't do this, Clara. It wouldn't be fair to your *suh*. He's been so brave, adjusting to an entirely new home and lifestyle. He's really *kumme* to love it here, even though he's counting down the days until you can be together permanently again. Don't do something rash now that might result in the two of you being separated for a much longer period of time."

Her back still turned, Clara didn't respond for several moments. Just when Josiah decided there was no sense in trying to get through to someone who was ignoring him, she asked, "Do you…do you really think Will's happy here?"

"I *know* he is," Josiah responded without hesitation. Nor did he give it a second thought before saying, "Your *schweschder* has seen to that. You couldn't have trusted him into the care of anyone more capable, loving and devoted than Anke is. I've seen how much she has joyfully sacrificed in order to provide a *hallich* home for Will until you can complete your program. And frankly, it would be selfish of you drop out of it now."

Clara broke out in tears, her shoulders heaving as she sobbed into her hands. "But I miss him so much…" Knowing that her loneliness was at the heart of her actions, Josiah kept quiet, allowing her time to weep. But meanwhile, he kept peering out the window, anxious that Anke and Will would return any minute.

When Clara's crying subsided, he said, "I can tell how much you love and miss your *suh*. And I can't imagine how difficult it is for the two of you to be separated. But you'll miss him even more if he's put into foster care for the long run."

She finally turned around and looked Josiah in the eye, nodding. "You're right—I know you're right. I shouldn't have *kumme* here. If Will sees me, it's going to make him lonely all over again when I leave. Could you give me a ride to the other side of town so I can meet my sponsor in the diner where none of the other Amish people in New Hope ever go? She'll pick me up and take me back to the center."

Josiah suppressed a groan. *I can just hear the rumors that will crop up if anyone sees me with another* Englisch *alcoholic,* he thought. But Clara was right; if Will saw her, it would be twice as hard for them to part a second time. *"Jah,"* he agreed. "But we'd better hurry."

"Just let me put Will's things back in the drawer." No sooner had she unzipped the duffel bag than a buggy came up the lane. "Oh, no! I can't let him see me! What am I going to do?"

Josiah's stomach lurched, but he said, "Quick—go into that room there and don't make a sound until Anke *kummes* to get you."

* * *

"Look! Josiah put in an extra step for me!" Will exclaimed as he and Anke approached the *daadi haus* and Velda and the other children walked in the opposite direction toward the main house.

"That's *wunderbaar*." Since Martha had dropped everyone off in the driveway, Anke hadn't been able to peek inside the barn to see if Josiah's buggy was there. But since the step was installed, she figured he'd left for the day.

However, just as they reached the porch, he stepped outside, closing the door behind him. "Hello. As you can see, I finished the last of my projects," he said cheerfully.

Anke scowled in response. *Why did he have to announce that? Couldn't he just have said goodbye as if it were any other day?* she silently carped. *Now Will is going want to go to—*

Even before she'd finished her thought, Will asked, "If you're all done, does that mean we get to go out for pizza?"

"We—we can't," Anke faltered. "Not today."

"Oh, that's right, your *bauch* probably still hurts, right?" Apparently, Josiah must have realized his blunder and he was trying to backpedal.

"*Jah*, it does." She pressed a hand against her abdomen.

"That's too bad, because I really had my heart set on pizza. Didn't you, Will?" Josiah asked, causing Anke to wonder if he was being spiteful or if he was really just obtuse. When her nephew agreed that he'd been looking forward to pizza, too, Josiah suggested, "I suppose you and I could go out—if your *ant* didn't mind staying home by herself?"

Will gave Anke a hopeful look. "Can we, *Ant* Anke?"

What in the world is Josiah thinking to suggest something like that in front of Will? Anke wondered. Yet she realized he'd actually come up with a perfect solution for avoiding being together, while also avoiding disappointing her nephew. *He doesn't want to hurt Will's feelings any more than I do...but what if the* bu *has such a great time that he grows even more attached to Josiah?*

As she was internally dithering, Josiah piped up again, "You know what, Will? We should give your *ant* a few minutes to make up her mind. I think I dropped some nails over there in the snow. Let's go see if we can find them while she comes to a decision." As he passed Anke on his way down the steps, he discreetly pressed a piece of paper into her hands.

She unfolded it to read, "Clara is inside the house. She'll explain everything. She doesn't want Will to see her." Anke gasped, her knees almost buckling beneath her.

Several yards away where he'd begun searching the snow for nails, Will jerked his head up. "What's wrong, *Ant* Anke?"

"My—my *bauch* feels really funny. I think you *buwe* should go ahead to the pizzeria without me."

"Denki!" Will cheered, charging forward to hug Anke before racing back to Josiah's side again.

"We won't be back until at least seven thirty. I promise," Josiah said with a pointed look that Anke took to mean he expected Clara would be gone by then.

"Okay. Have *schpass*." She held on to the porch railing to steady herself as she watched them disappear into the barn. She waited in that position until she saw Josiah's buggy pull out into the driveway and down the lane. Then she darted up the stairs and into the house. She didn't see her sister in the living room, but when she flung open the bedroom door, Clara dove into her arms.

"Oh, Anke," she cried. "I almost made a huge mistake—*again*."

"*Kumme*, sit with me in the living room and tell me all about it."

So her sister spent the next hour pouring out her heart. She told Anke how much she missed Will, what a struggle it had been to stop drinking and how ashamed she felt for making such poor choices and causing everyone so much pain. In turn, Anke recounted everything she could think of that Will had done since he'd come to live with them, including singing "The *Loblied*" in church. She reminded Clara of Christ's love and forgiveness for everyone who chose to put their faith in Him. And she encouraged her to stick with the recovery program.

"I have no intention of quitting again," Clara assured her. "Although now I'll probably have to stay an extra week or two because I'll have to start over from the beginning. Is it okay if Will stays with you a little longer?"

"Don't be *lappich*. Of course he can!"

Clara checked the time on her cell phone. She had called Yolanda almost forty-five minutes earlier, so she projected if they left now they'd arrive at the diner at about the same time as her sponsor did. "Even if we get there a little early, it's better if I go before Will returns, otherwise, I might not be able to leave at all."

Anke refrained from saying that was her exact wish: for them both to stay in New Hope permanently. The last thing she wanted was for her sister to feel trapped or pressured. Clara was already extremely emotional. "I'll go tell Ernest I'm taking the buggy. Don't worry— I'll be discreet."

"Can you…can you ask him to *kumme* out for a minute? I'd like to say hello."

So their brother met them in the barn, where he and Clara shared such a sweet embrace that Anke had to turn away, for fear she'd start crying.

Once the sisters arrived at the diner, they chatted in the buggy until they spotted Yolanda's car turning into the parking lot.

"*Denki* for everything you're doing for me and Will," Clara said, giving Anke a good-bye hug. "As Josiah said, I'd never find anyone more loving, capable and devoted to care for my *suh*."

"Josiah said that?"

"Yeah. I can tell he thinks the world of you." Clara pulled back to look her in the eye. "Tell me the truth. He's your suitor, isn't he?"

"*Neh*. He's not."

"That's too bad. He's the kind of man I wish I had chosen. He seems like he'd be a really positive role model for a young boy like Will."

The first thing Anke did after her sister and Yolanda drove away was to bow her head and thank the Lord that Clara had decided to return to the recovery program, and to ask Him to give her strength to start over again. On the way home, Anke's thoughts turned to her sister's observation about Josiah. He really had gone out of his way to protect Will from getting his feelings hurt tonight—both by encouraging Clara to return to her recovery program and by taking Will out for pizza as he'd promised. Nothing about Josiah's behavior or what he'd said to her sister indicated that he resented Anke's commitment to her family.

Maybe I misjudged him. It's possible that he just reacted poorly in the moment on Sunndaag *because he was disappointed I decided not to go snowshoeing,* she thought. *And Clara herself said she'd like Will to have someone like Josiah for a role model. So maybe we don't have to keep our distance from him after all.*

If her sister had the courage to admit her mistakes and try again in her recovery program, then with God's help, Anke was going to try again with Josiah, too. The question was, did *he* want to start anew with her?

Josiah softly rapped on the door of the *daadi haus* so he wouldn't wake Will, who was asleep in his arms. They had returned later than he'd expected because they'd stopped at the apparel store before going to the pizzeria so Josiah could buy the boy a hat similar to his own. He supposed he should have asked Anke if it was okay first. But he figured she wouldn't be opposed to him giving the boy a traditional Amish piece of clothing as a gift. In any case, they'd gotten to the pizzeria later than he'd intended and it was very crowded, so they'd had to wait for a booth. By the time they'd finished their meal, Will was so full and tired that he'd fallen asleep in the buggy on the way home.

Anke was smiling when she opened the door. "Hello, *buwe*—" she started to stay. But when she saw that her nephew was sleeping, she covered her mouth and whispered, "Oops, sorry."

She gestured for Josiah to follow her into Will's newly finished bedroom. He laid the boy down on his cot and then helped Anke remove his shoes and coat. After they'd tiptoed into the living room, Anke held up the hat and asked incredulously, "You got this for him?"

"*Jah.*" Josiah stiffened his spine. "I didn't think you'd object."

Anke wrinkled her forehead. "Why would I object? It was very thoughtful...like so many things you've done for us. Especially tonight." She took a step closer and looked him squarely in the eyes. "I can't thank you enough for encouraging Clara to return to the recovery program and for keeping Will from discovering she'd been here."

Josiah brushed off her compliment, saying, "There's no need to thank me. I did it for her *suh*." He reached for the doorknob, but before turning it, he remarked over his shoulder, "Since you don't want to associate with me anymore, you can put my final paycheck in the mail once you have a chance to write it out. I also left the receipts for the materials I bought on top of the fridge."

"Wait!" Anke placed her hand over his. Her touch was gentle and warm. "I never said I didn't want to associate with you—I said it wasn't a *gut* idea for us to socialize, but I didn't mean forever. I only meant while Will was here. Even so, I made a mistake and I'm very sorry."

Josiah slid his hand out from under hers and dropped it to his side. Facing her, he asked, "You're sorry—what changed your mind? Did the deacon set the record straight with you, too, like he did with Keith Harnish?"

Anke scrunched up her face and tipped her head in what appeared to be genuine bafflement. "Iddo Stoll? Keith Harnish? What do either of them have to do with my decision about whether to socialize with you?"

Now Josiah was perplexed. "I—I thought I heard Keith telling you about the video of me getting caught with alcohol in the back of my buggy. Isn't that why you wanted to distance yourself from me?"

"*Neh*, of course not. As I told you, I didn't think it was *gut* for Will to get the idea we were a couple. You saw the picture he'd drawn of us holding hands... I was afraid he was beginning to feel like we were replacing his *mamm* and *daed*. Or that he was growing too attached to you, in particular. I didn't want to make it harder for him to leave when the time came."

"But Keith *did* tell you about the video, right?"

"*Jah*. But I assumed that was just a case of mistaken identity."

As relieved as Josiah was that he'd been wrong about Anke's motivation for not wanting to socialize with him, he realized she might change her mind again when he told her what had really happened at the golf course. But it was important to him to know whether she trusted he was telling the truth, so he admitted, "It wasn't a case of mistaken identity. It really was me in the video clip. But the beer in the buggy wasn't mine. I've never had a drop of alcohol in my—"

Anke interrupted. "You don't have to explain. I believe you. I told Keith that, too—I said you'd never break your commitment to abide by the *Ordnung*." She scowled as she added, "I think he was part of the reason I had a *koppweh* that afternoon."

Josiah's legs felt weak when he realized how wrong he'd been about her, so he asked if they could sit down. Anke perched on the edge of the rocker and he took a seat facing her in Will's armchair. Leaning forward on his knees, he peered into her eyes and confessed, "I'm the one who made a mistake—I wrongly assumed that *you* believed a lie about me. That's why I got so upset after *kurrich* on *Sunndaag*. I'm sorry for how immaturely I behaved. I should have heard you out instead of storming off, but I was defensive because…because of things that happened in my past."

Anke's face blossomed with a smile. "That's okay. I was defensive, too. I assumed you were angry because I was putting my *familye*'s needs above my desire to have *schpass* with you."

"Are you kidding me? Your commitment to your *familye* is one of the qualities I appreciate the most in you." Josiah sat up straighter.

"I feel very blessed to have been part of your *familye*'s life. And I'd really like to continue to hang out with you and Will…but aren't you still concerned he'll grow too attached to me?"

"*Neh.* Not since Clara mentioned that she wished Will had a role model like you in his life. That's when I realized that even if he only knows you for a short amount of time, the influence you have on him now could last his entire life. Besides, a *kind* can never have too much love. And the fact of the matter is, he's *already* grown attached to you."

"I've grown attached to him, too." Josiah gazed into her sea-green eyes, adding softly, "And to you, Anke."

Her voice barely a whisper, she replied, "I feel the same way about you, too."

Josiah took her hand in his. "Then will you accept me as your suitor?"

"*Jah.*" She gently squeezed his fingers. "As long as it's okay if Will sometimes comes with us when we go out?"

"Sure. He can be our chaperone—to make sure we don't do too much of this." Josiah leaned forward and gave her a soft, lingering kiss.

"In that case, forget I asked," Anke teased. "He can stay home with his *gschwischderkinner.*"

Epilogue

⟋

"I can't believe you're actually moving out," Clara said to Anke as she helped her pack. The sisters and Will had been living in the *daadi haus* together for a little over a year and a half, ever since Clara completed her recovery program and returned to New Hope. But tomorrow was Anke's wedding. After that, she'd live with Josiah in the house he'd built on property he'd bought from his brother. "How will I ever manage without you?"

"You'll do just fine," Anke assured her. In the past year, she had witnessed her sister growing more and more responsible, mature and faithful to the baptismal commitment she'd made to God and her Amish community. "*I'm* the one who's going to feel lost without you and Will."

"*Gott* willing, soon enough you'll have *bob-*

blin of your own to care for—and you'll have your own *haus*, too. You'll forget all about us. You know what they say—out of sight, out of mind."

"*Neh*, that's not true," Anke insisted somberly, even though she recognized that her sister had only been teasing. "The entire time you were gone, you were never out of my mind, Clara. You were always in my prayers. And as far as having *bobblin* of my own… I hope I do. But that won't change how much I love Will or any of my nieces and nephews. Or you."

"I know it won't," Clara replied just as seriously. Then she smiled a playful smile. "Do you think your *bobblin* will have hair like Josiah's?"

Before Anke could answer, the two women heard footsteps on the porch. They went into the living room just as Josiah and Will entered from outside. They both wore identical hats, which they swept off their heads and hung on two pegs by the door. Although Will's peg was lower than Josiah's, he no longer had to stand on tiptoe to reach it, the way he did two months ago.

"I'm *hungerich*," the boy announced. "May I have *kuchen,* please?"

After Clara took him into the kitchen to give him warm milk and a cookie, Josiah asked,

"Did I hear someone saying my name when I walked in?"

"We were just talking about your hair." Anke stepped closer to him and reached up to finger a curl.

"You mean my rooster's comb?" he asked.

Anke laughed, remembering what Millie had said the first time she'd seen Josiah's vivid red spirals. "I love your hair."

Josiah encircled her waist and pulled her a little nearer. "I love your turtle-blue eyes," he joked, using Will's word for *turquoise*. "But not as much as I love your ears."

"My ears? But they stick out."

"Exactly. It makes them easier to kiss." He demonstrated several times, which tickled and made Anke giggle so hard that she was afraid Will and Clara would return to the room to see what was so funny.

"Absatz," she whispered.

"Okay, I will," he agreed reluctantly. "But I'm only going to keep my word about that until tomorrow, when we're married…"

* * * * *

*If you enjoyed this story by Carrie Lighte,
be sure to pick up the previous books in
The Amish of New Hope miniseries:*

Hiding Her Amish Secret
An Unexpected Amish Harvest

Available now from Love Inspired!

*And look for more Amish romances every
month from Love Inspired!*

Dear Reader,

Although my Amish romance novels are entirely fictitious, lately my imagination has been sparked by reading my favorite Amish newspaper. The publication is composed mostly of letters written by Amish and Mennonite "scribes," across the country, who provide news about the weather, births, deaths and social activities in their areas. Often, these reports contain accounts of accidents, injuries and illnesses, too. They're also highlighted with humorous anecdotes and words of encouragement in the Lord.

In some ways, the publication reminds me of social media but without any of the negative kind of news that can be found online among *Englischers*. For example, no one would ever submit an article about what happened to Josiah at the golf course. This isn't to imply that Amish people don't gossip among themselves, since gossiping is a temptation for all of us. But in general, the newspaper is informative and uplifting, like correspondence from a family member or a good friend.

Speaking of keeping in touch, I love hearing from *you*, too, so please don't hesitate to drop me a line.

Blessings,
Carrie Lighte

Get 4 FREE REWARDS!

We'll send you 2 FREE Books plus 2 FREE Mystery Gifts.

Love Inspired books feature uplifting stories where faith helps guide you through life's challenges and discover the promise of a new beginning.

FREE Value Over $20